LEAVE IT TO
CHRISTY

D0483621

Pamela Curtis Swallow

SCHOLASTIC INC.
New York Toronto London Auckland Sydney

ISBN 0-590-41666-9

12 11 10 9 8 7 6 5 4 3 2 1 8 9/8 0 1 2 3/9

Printed in the U.S.A. 11

First Scholastic printing, August 1988

To Corrie and to Paula Danziger

One

Right 25 . . . left 16 . . . right 4 . . . Pull. "Uh-oh." Right 25 . . . left 16 . . . right 4 . . . Tug. "Shoot." Right 25 . . . left 16 . . . right 4 . . . Yank. Kick. "Oh, great. Late again."

"You got problems?" Mr. Johnson, the custodian, stood behind me. He smelled of fuel oil.

I leaned against the wall of lockers and gave hateful old number 66 one last whack with the heel of my sneaker. A bell rang and the hallway quickly cleared. I moaned and sagged to the floor. I felt like a puny, pathetic heap of loser.

"My locker," I said. "I can't get it open . . . AGAIN." A headache was pushing up the back of my neck.

"Middle-school lockers take getting used to," Mr. Johnson said, smiling.

"They told us that Wednesday. But this is Friday and

the teachers aren't going to let me be late much longer." I had to turn away so he couldn't see my eyes blurring.

"I'll open it for you, Christy. Watch." He wiped his hands on his pants and began to turn the knob. "You'll get the hang of it."

I'll bet he knew the names of only two seventh graders so far—me, and the kid who threw up in the hall yesterday. I pressed my top teeth into my bottom lip as I watched him open it with ease.

Thanking Mr. Johnson, I grabbed my science and math books and slammed the locker with such force that the hall seemed to shake. A teacher stuck her head out her classroom door and glared.

This year was definitely not starting the way I had imagined it would. In elementary school I'd been a big cheese. Here I was a dumb little nothing.

To make up time, I skidded around the corner and tore down the hall. But I was still late for science. Frogface Abbot looked up at me through his safety goggles.

"Locker again, Ms. Swan?" he said, neither smiling nor frowning.

"Yes, sorry. I almost have it, though." I imagined him eating flies.

"Almost? It either opens or it doesn't."

"Well, I feel that I'm getting closer," I answered, squeezing between desks, stepping over books and bags, knocking Beth Roman's purse to the floor, and finally stumbling into my seat. My best friend, Lizzie, gave me a sympathetic smile.

Frogface didn't. He sighed and looked down at the glass containers in front of him. "Now that we are, at last, all here, we can continue this demonstration." He mixed and poured, explaining that elements and compounds were changing, and remarking that it was all very interesting.

Maybe there was something the matter with me. I didn't find it interesting at all.

As he cleaned up his mixtures, Mr. Abbot gave us the terrible news. "We are now going to spend some time talking about your first science project for the term. Each of you is to work independently, I repeat, INDEPENDENTLY, on a project of your choosing. You must, however, have your topic approved by me."

There went any possibility of its being bearable, I thought. If Lizzie and I were allowed to work together, it might not be too bad.

"Forty percent of your grade for the marking period," he continued, "will depend on this project. I know that you will derive much satisfaction from learning to use the scientific method and from doing truly INDEPENDENT thinking. You will discover that there is no better way to understand what real science is all about." He paused and smiled long and hard at us. I noticed a big smudge of chalk dust on the arm of his jacket. "Now, if you will, let's talk about some possible subjects you might like to explore."

Or might *not* like to explore, I thought.

"I am going to pass out a list of the more successful ones done in previous years."

"Skip the list. Just pass out," I mumbled, giggling to myself.

Mr. Abbot had taken off his safety goggles. Red dents circled each eye.

The list was scary, complicated, and just plain awful:

Conductors and insulators
Crystals
One-celled animals
Osmosis and diffusion
Photosynthesis
Digestive organs of chickens . . .

That last one explained the smell in the science lab.

The sound of finger tapping made me look up. The boy next to me, Michael Somebody, was drumming a kind of rhythm on his desk with his thin fingers. He didn't seem to be paying attention to anything that had been going on. As the pile of lists reached him, he just handed them along to the person behind him, without even taking one. Boy, he must have figured the project was even more hopeless than I did. At least I made the appearance of being interested. I didn't dare not.

If it weren't for the finger tapping, he could pass for an understuffed mannequin dressed in dirty old clothes and propped up to fill a space in the row.

"I guess this isn't your favorite subject either," I couldn't help whispering to him.

He didn't answer. What was with this kid? He just slouched in his chair and looked out the window.

Mr. Abbot cleared his throat so I decided I'd better drop the so far one-sided conversation. He started in again. "By Monday you must present your topics. That gives you the weekend to consider what you'd like to investigate. I'm sure you will become interested, even fascinated, as you probe further into your subject." Mr. Abbot's eyes glistened.

I knew I was in trouble. I couldn't think of a single

science topic I wanted to probe. There was a big gap between how much Mr. Abbot cared and how much I cared about science. Now, if he asked me to write a poem, or play, or short story, or anything creative like that, I'd have been on my way. I love to write. In fact, I like just about everything . . . except science . . . and liver.

I gazed across the room at Jeffrey Matthews. Now there's something worth investigating, I thought. Cute face, brown eyes, dark wavy hair . . . but Mr. Abbot wouldn't approve that topic. Jeff was studying the list and writing in his notebook. He probably had good ideas spilling out all over. It figured. Not only was he gorgeous, but, with my luck, he was a future scientist. It was going to be hard to impress him.

"Mr. Abbot, would comparing the body systems of a frog and a toad be a good project?" Eric Sutton asked.

"The idea is fine, Eric, but I seem to recall that it was done a couple of years ago by a student named Kimberly Sutton. She wouldn't be any relation of yours, would she?" Mr. Abbot stared sharply at Eric.

"Uh, I do have a sister. I'm not sure what project she did though," Eric said softly.

"How about the social lives of insects?" asked Beth Roman. "I read somewhere that many insects really have social communication."

"That project has possibilities. Think it over and give me the details on Monday, Beth."

By the end of the period I had a stomachache from listening to kids discussing science-project ideas. I could think of absolutely nothing. Zero.

Lizzie didn't look especially happy either, but at least

she didn't look the way I felt—queasy, about to throw up. Her long, thin legs were stretched out into the aisle beside her and her scowl told me that wheels were turning inside. What was the matter with me? Flat tire?

The rest of my afternoon classes were a blur. It was a shame too, because I usually like math and reading. But Old Frogface had spoiled them.

At three o'clock, standing in front of my one hundred percent locked locker again, I thought of going home and getting a sledgehammer to bash the thing to bits. I glanced out the hall window and saw Michael What's-his-name trudging across the grass. He must have been the first one out the door. Either he was having locker problems too, or he didn't do homework, because he wasn't carrying any books.

When I finally hit the jackpot and got old number 66 open, the halls were nearly empty. It would have been nice if a few people I knew could have witnessed my triumph.

Way down at the eighth grade end of the hall, I could see my sister, Sarah, with a bunch of her snobby friends. They were talking and laughing, probably about how immature seventh graders were. I was pretty sure one of those girls, the one with the top of her hair permed like a head of broccoli, had seen me racing down the hall late for class. By now my sister was enjoying the news.

Lizzie came out of the band room. "Hi, Christy. Wait a minute. I had to get the valves of my trumpet oiled. I'll be ready in a second."

"Liz," I said, as I looked out the double door. "Whatever made me think middle school would be so great?" I could see the roof of my old elementary school in the distance. "I'm sure I heard somewhere these are supposed to be the best years of our lives . . . why would anyone say that?"

"Beats me," said Lizzie with a shrug.

Down the hall, Sarah let out a snort of laughter.

Two

The house smelled like meat loaf. Dad must have cooked it in the afternoon. We all like it better cold than hot. Dad's a writer and works at home most of the time. He was in the kitchen when we walked in.

"Well, ladies, how does it feel to have finished your first week of school? It's nice how the first week is a short one. You can e–a–s–e back into it," Dad said cheerfully as he dried four potatoes and set them by the oven.

Sarah was already pigging out on cookies and managed only a mumble. She holds the record for the fastest time from the front door to the cookie jar. It's an automatic reflex of hers—open door, sprint to jar. And she never gains a pound.

"Hey, go easy on those cookies," warned Dad.

"Dad," I said, "what do you know about science?"

"Well, I took science just like everyone else, and I keep up with what's in the news. Why?"

"Oh, we have to do an independent project in science, that's all. I thought you might have some ideas." I tried to sound casual. There was no point in letting everyone see how panicked I was.

Sarah looked up. "Ah-ha! The famous Abbot science projects. They're killers. Wait'll you get to his favorite—the bug collection."

"We have a choice," I said.

"You do now. You won't then. Everyone has to do it. Enjoy your choice while you can. By the way, you should start collecting bugs. Once it begins to get cold, they're hard to find." Sarah knew how to make a depressed person feel better.

"Dad, what about in the good old days, when you were in school? Were there science projects back then?" I asked.

"Even in the dark ages, we had science projects. I remember my praying mantis project. I was about your age when I found a nest, or egg sac. I put it in a jar and brought it to school. I read up on how the babies hatch and grow, and I planned to tell the class all about it, while it was happening, sort of a play-by-play. Well, I had that jar sitting in my desk, and not much happened. I figured the nest was a dud.

"But one morning I came to school, opened my desk, and discovered it was crawling with praying mantises! The jar lid hadn't been on tight and they all escaped. A few minutes later my teacher arrived. She wasn't too fond of bugs, at least not by the hundreds. I didn't get much credit for that project," Dad said, laughing.

I was not encouraged.

I went to my room to talk to Hazel. She's my plant. I

won her at a school fair three years ago and we've been friends ever since. She's not a beauty—no real flowers or anything, just green leaves—but I like her. She has an easy personality and she's a good listener. I flopped on my bed. "Trouble, Hazel. Serious trouble. I have a science project and don't have a topic. Any ideas?" Hazel listened quietly. "I think I'm doomed."

I sat up and looked in the mirror. Ugh. Mousy, wavy hair, freckles, a retainer in my mouth, no real figure. I thought of Jeff, the only good thing about science class, and I knew I wasn't going to dazzle him with either my remarkable knowledge or my striking good looks.

Cute. I have been described as cute for as long as I can remember. Sarah doesn't get called cute. Beautiful, lovely, gorgeous are more like it. Somehow cute seems to be a runner-up word.

What project did Sarah-the-sensational do for Mr. Abbot?

Sarah was reading on her bed when I walked into her room. "You didn't knock," she said.

"The door was open."

"My room is still off limits to you, unless you have permission," she muttered, not looking up.

I ignored her comment and went on with my question. "What science projects did you do in seventh grade?"

"As soon as you go out and knock, I'll tell you."

"That's dumb," I said, but I stomped out, knocked and came back in.

She took her time before answering. "Okay. Plant growth was the first one. Remember all those cups with little plants in them all along the windowsills? I was investigating the effects of different lights."

"Mainly I remember that some of the plants rotted and stank. And it was boring."

"It was, pretty much. But Mr. Abbot liked it." Sarah smiled as she recalled another of her many good grades.

"He won't like mine. I can't think of a single thing to do. I'll fail," I said, sitting down hard on the edge of her bed.

"The class is murder—you'll be lucky to get through it alive. But Mr. Abbot's not really such a bad guy. Why are you all worked up about homework on Friday? You don't have to worry until Sunday night."

That's typical of Sarah. She never worries about school, always puts off major assignments until the last minute, and still manages to get good marks. Teachers love her. So do boys.

"Does that guy, Billy Matthews, who's in your jazz-rock band, have a younger brother, Jeff?" I tried to sound casual.

"Umm, I think so. Yes, I saw him once at Billy's house. Why?"

"Nothing. He's in my science class."

"And he's cute, right?" Sarah smiled at me.

"Why do you think that?"

"You're so obvious, Chris."

"No, I'm not." I sighed and went back to my room. "Well, Hazel, things are no better. But I have to prove to Sarah that I can handle it." Hazel agreed. She always does.

That night at dinner Sarah made a point of mentioning the fact that she'd heard that the janitor had to help me open my locker.

"He's helped lots of kids." I glared at Sarah. "Anyway, I'm getting the hang of it now."

"You've perfected your technique?" Mom said, smiling. She and Dad weren't making fun, but I could see that they thought it was amusing. Sometimes it's a pain being an amusing person.

"I've decided to show the locker who's boss. I give it a kick before I try to open it. That worked this afternoon . . . eventually."

"Chris," Dad said, "maybe Mom had better luck with her science projects than I had. She might have an idea or two."

"Oh, Lord, here we go again," Mom said. "I remember Sarah's bugs. Some things change from year to year, but not Mr. Abbot, it seems."

"Did you have to do a school science project, Mom?"

"Well, I remember doing something with hamsters and a maze once for a science fair."

I liked hamsters. Maybe Mom could help.

"But it was dreadful, and not very scientific," she went on. "The first hamster died and I had to substitute another halfway through the experiment. Then I got sick and your Uncle Bill helped out, but he didn't really know what I was trying to show. Things got pretty muddled. It was not a Nobel Prize–winning project."

Maybe Mom couldn't help.

Being bad at science must be hereditary. It was obvious I had a severe shortage of science genes. Of course, Sarah was spared.

The phone rang. It was Lizzie asking me to come over on Saturday. I had play tryouts in the morning, but Mom and Dad nodded that the afternoon was fine. Sarah and I are in a drama group which meets several days a week. We are almost always involved in some play.

"What are you going to do this weekend, Sarah?" Mom asked.

"After tryouts tomorrow, I'm meeting a bunch of kids from school at the mall to shop and see a movie. Then tomorrow night I'm sitting for the Simpsons . . ." Sarah went on. She always had plenty of plans. No shortage there.

Dad got up to clear the table. "Whose turn is it to load the dishwasher?"

"Christy's," Sarah said. "I set the table and fed Beezer." At the sound of her name, Beezer, our golden retriever, thumped her tail under the table. One reason we all love her so much is that she mostly just lies around, thumping and smiling. I know dogs aren't supposed to be able to smile, but ours definitely does. We got her from an eighty-two-year-old lady who said that she wanted a dog with more spunk. My parents said that any dog too calm for an eighty-two-year-old lady is just the dog for them. Beezer and Hazel have a lot in common. If I was going to be a science dud and a seventh-grade zero, then maybe I had a lot in common with Beezer and Hazel, too.

Three

Test tubes, one-celled animals, and chicken organs kept bobbing in front of me as I lay in bed that night. Saturday morning, still tired, I shuffled down to breakfast. Sparkling Sarah was talking to Dad about the roles she would be trying out for. The play was *Peter Pan* and she wanted to be Wendy. Mrs. Darling was her second choice. I knew she'd be good at either. If she weren't so mature and feminine, I figured she'd be trying out for Peter.

"Hi, Chris. How're you doing?" Dad asked.

"Ugh."

"Too bad. What role are you auditioning for this morning?" he asked as he got up to pour himself another mug of coffee.

"Don't know. Haven't decided. Probably an Indian or a lost boy," I answered unenthusiastically. I looked to see what Sarah was eating. Disgustingly sweet, syrup-soaked waffles. They made the kitchen smell sick.

"You're a better actress than you give yourself credit for, you know that?" Dad said encouragingly. "Once you get going and throw yourself into something, you're great. Your energy and enthusiasm are contagious."

"Thanks." I pushed a couple of stale slices of bread into the toaster, then leaned against the counter waiting for them to be done. Looking between the calico curtains on the window, I could see sparrows and finches in the crabapple tree. We always have a lot of birds around. Birdhouses, bird feeders, suet, berry bushes, and fruit trees make the Swan house a year-round favorite fast-food spot. I wouldn't be surprised if we had a partridge in our pear tree. Be kind to your fine feathered friends, I hummed to myself. With Swan for my last name, a duck *could* be my uncle. I'd been called a birdbrain more than once.

Dad drove us to auditions. As we pulled into the lot, he handed me some change so I could call him when I was done. Sociable Sarah was getting a ride directly to the mall with friends.

"Good luck and have fun!" Dad called as he putted off in his VW bug.

In the old Forum Theater, George, our director who's been running the youth drama program for years, had some older students signing in the kids who were auditioning. George's productions are so good that he never has a problem getting a cast and crew. Kids who start with George when they're young usually stick with him right up through high school.

A few adults I didn't know, probably some of George's

New York theater friends, were getting themselves organized at what looked like the casting directors' table. Over against one wall, George's college-age daughter was warming up on the piano. She's usually the accompanist for auditions, then George gets someone to take over and do it for the play.

"All you kids trying out, take seats in the audience after you've signed in. Make sure you give us your phone numbers, because we may be calling you. All right, now. We'll call your names one by one. If you know a song from *Peter Pan*, sing it. Otherwise sing one from another show."

My stomach turned icy as I took a seat near the back. Even though I knew a lot of kids, I wanted to sit and tremble alone. But not never-nervous Sarah—she was sitting ahead of me with friends, bright-eyed and confident.

Auditions began. Why do I do this to myself? I could have been at Lizzie's having fun. Instead, I put myself through this ordeal. My knees shake, my voice cracks, and my stomach would rather be anywhere else. Is it worth it? Well, yes. Once this awful part is over, it is. I really like working with a cast and crew on a production. The teamwork makes everyone feel close. And the feeling of being part of a great show is exciting.

One of Sarah's friends was called. She was trying for the part of Wendy, and she wasn't too bad. Her voice sounded kind of shrill, but she had the right look. Sarah chewed on a nail as she watched, then gave her returning friend a pat on the shoulder.

A boy named Stanley tried out for Captain Hook and was excellent. He made all of us laugh, including the casting directors and the accompanist. There wasn't much doubt about his getting the role. He was experienced and had even acted in New York.

"Nice job, Stanley," George called from the back of the theater. "That sinister-looking mustache added something."

When Sarah was called, I crossed my fingers. She looked comfortable on stage and her voice sounded relaxed. I glanced around the audience and saw that everyone was watching her closely. George liked working with Sarah. She was reliable and always listened to his instructions. Directors, like teachers, go for kids who keep still and pay attention.

A few more kids were called. I twisted an unraveled thread hanging from my shirt as I watched future pirates, Indians, and lost boys try to look the parts. A couple of kids tried out for Peter Pan.

When my name was called, I pushed myself up with my sweaty hands and wobbled up to the stage on trembling legs. I thought I heard Sarah whisper, "Good luck."

"Hi, Chris," George said. "What role?"

"Umm . . . I guess an Indian. I'll sing the 'Ugg-A-Wugg' song." I knew all the songs from the show, because ever since I'd been little, I'd listened to Mom's Mary Martin record of the Broadway play.

The piano began and after a few notes I joined in, kind of softly at first. Then I got the nerve to look at George. He smiled, so I sang louder. The adults at the table smiled too, so I got even louder and began to move around the stage a bit. George signaled the piano to stop, and then he walked to the table. Uh-oh, I'd blown it.

"Chris, do you know 'I Gotta Crow,' or any of Peter's songs?" George asked.

I nodded.

"Okay, try 'I Gotta Crow,' please."

The piano played the introduction and I was off. I remembered how Mary Martin had done the song with spirit, and with steadily growing confidence, I began to throw myself into it. One of the casting directors leaned across the table to speak to the others. I thought I'd lost their attention. Peter was cocky and conceited, and would never have been able to stand being ignored. So I leaped down from the stage and strutted, still singing, right up to the table. Arching backward, I tossed my head back so that I was practically looking them upside down in the face, kicked up one foot, and sang about "the cleverness of the remarkable me." Chuckles encouraged me. I skipped over to the piano, leaned one elbow on it, and winked at the accompanist. Then, at the final dramatic moment, I hopped up next to her on the piano bench and belted out my crows.

I looked out into the audience and saw the startled faces. My own face suddenly reddened as I glanced toward the rear of the room and saw Sarah looking embarrassed. I guess to say I'd overdone it would be a huge understatement. I couldn't believe I'd let go as much as I had. I jumped down from the bench and ran to get my things.

"Oh, God, Christy. What's the matter with you?" Sarah said angrily as I hurried by.

"Don't know," I answered, fumbling for my jacket. "I'm calling Dad. I don't want to watch the rest."

"'Bye," she snapped, looking away.

I rammed the door at the back of the theater and felt it smack into something. Peering behind the door, I was startled to see Michael, the finger tapper from school, standing there looking a little dazed.

"Oh, I'm sorry."

"It's okay," he answered, rubbing his forehead.

"I didn't see you. You all right?" I must have whacked him pretty hard.

"Yeah. No problem."

I stooped to look for the quarter that had flown out of my hand. "Oh, great. Now I've lost my money."

Michael leaned down, picked up the coin by his sneaker, and handed it to me. "You weren't bad in there."

"Oh, please." I rolled my eyes. "But thanks, anyway."

He shrugged.

What was he doing at the theater, anyway?

I was quiet in the car on the way to Lizzie's, keeping my fiasco to myself. I didn't even look at Dad; he'd said he liked energy and enthusiasm, but this audition may have gone beyond that into dynamo and frenzy. Why did I let myself get so carried away?

Was it possible, I wondered, to make a complete fool of myself in front of thirty or forty people without the whole world finding out?

Monday would be a disaster.

Four

Not judging people is one of Lizzie's nicest qualities. So is the fact that she can keep a secret. But I knew that my audition would not be a secret once Monday morning rolled around. Lizzie would stick up for me when she heard people say what an idiot I'd been, and it would be easier for her if she had some background. So when I got to her house, I explained what had happened. Lizzie just listened and smiled, then said, "Well, at least you were enthusiastic. Throwing yourself into what you do can be good. A lot of people never really get into anything."

"I more than threw myself—I hurtled, catapulted, did a Swan dive."

Lizzie chuckled at my very small Swan joke. "I'm sure you were really good, and certainly more fun to watch than most of the kids."

"Thanks. Well, whatever . . . it's too late now."

Lizzie and I have been friends since we were six.

Until this year, when the three elementary schools emptied into one middle school, we hadn't even been in the same school. Ever since we met in a swim class, back when we were "polliwogs" at the YMCA, we've stayed buddies. It's been worth the extra work it took to keep in touch all those years.

Lizzie's family is a lot like ours in many ways, except they're taller. I mean TALL. We're not shrimpy. In fact, we're probably taller than average. But they're taller. Lizzie's already taller than Mom, and her feet are bigger than Sarah's.

Once we got done discussing my botched tryouts, we moved on to the subject of school and kids in our classes. I asked her if she'd noticed Jeff Matthews.

"I've known him for years. He's our paperboy. We used to carpool to school when we were at Stevenson."

It's weird that now that we're in middle school, there are loads of kids Lizzie knows that I don't, and lots I know that she doesn't, and a bunch neither of us knows.

"What time does your paper come?"

"About twenty minutes from now," Lizzie said. She got up from the front steps. "I'll get some cards." She came back with an Oreo sticking out of her mouth. More were in her hand, stacked on top of the deck of cards. "Want some?"

I shook my head.

"Let's play rummy," she said calmly.

My stomach was beginning to flip-flop. "Maybe we shouldn't sit here," I said.

"We should if you want to talk to him. Don't you want to?" Lizzie dealt the cards.

"Yes and no."

"Which most?"

"Yes."

"Well, then, this is the place to be. He leaves the paper right here," Lizzie said, patting the step matter-of-factly. "Go ahead, it's your turn." The cards slapped on the wood. I kept glancing down Lizzie's driveway. My mind was not on the game. "I won," Lizzie said, laying her cards down in neat groups.

The crunch of gravel startled me. I froze. Jeff was coming up the long driveway on his bike. His head was down, concentrating on peddling through the places where the gravel had bunched together. I stood up and began to back slowly toward the door. Then I saw Jeff look up. I was stuck. It would look pretty stupid if I left now. I thought I saw his face turning red, but it was hard to tell with his tan. What little tan I'd gotten over the summer, (which wasn't really so much a tan as it was more freckles) was on the fade. But Jeff had perfect skin.

"Hi, Jeff," chirped Lizzie.

"Hi," he answered, looking down into his bag of newspapers and digging for a pad. "I'm collecting today. It's a dollar seventy."

"My folks aren't here, but I'll look for some money," Liz said, hopping up and going inside. I was stranded outside. I didn't know where to look or what to say. I stared at his bike. It was black and yellow.

"Nice bike," I finally said weakly.

"Thanks." Jeff looked toward the door. I was sure he couldn't wait for Lizzie to come out and rescue him. I watched the door too. How long was she going to stay in there?

"How's your locker coming?" he finally said.

"My locker? Oh, I think it hates me."

Jeff smiled and finally looked away from the door and toward me. Oh, God he's cute, I thought. I tried to smile, but it felt crooked. Oh, jeez! My retainer was in. It must look stupid. Where was Lizzie anyway? I looked back toward the door and felt so dumb not talking. My sister never had this problem—she was always chatting and laughing.

One time I read that you should find out what a boy is interested in, then talk about that. Why hadn't I asked Lizzie more about him before I got into this? Science. I remembered him looking interested in science (God knows why).

"So," I said, trying to sound casual, "what are you going to do your science project on?"

"I think I'll study magnetism and electricity. Probably I'll build an electromagnet and a few other things."

"Sounds good," I commented stupidly. I wanted to say something intelligent, but I knew next to nothing about electromagnets. No, make that nothing.

"Here y'go," Liz said, letting the screen door bang behind her. She handed Jeff two dollars. "It took me a while to find the money." She sounded ridiculously cheery. "My parents tip you, right? Keep the change."

"Thanks," he said, stuffing the bills into his pants pocket. "See you." He peddled down the drive, and I watched his back grow smaller until he disappeared around the hedge.

"Oh, rats! I blew it!" I smacked my hand hard on the step. "Where were you, anyway?"

"What do you mean, 'where'? I was inside trying to find money, that's where." Lizzie was trying to sound innocent.

"You were gone for ages. I didn't have anything to say. He thinks I'm a total jerk."

"I doubt that, Chris."

"This year stinks!" I spat out my retainer and flung it across the yard.

Later, Lizzie's mother drove me home. When we pulled into our driveway, I saw a piece of paper taped to the front door. Instantly I thought it must say something awful, such as that my whole family was in the hospital and I should go to a neighbor's.

I ran up to it. Big green letters said, WELCOME HOME, PETER PAN!

I stared at the sign.

"What's it say?" Lizzie called from the car.

"I don't believe it," I called back over my shoulder. "It says, 'Welcome home, Peter Pan!' "

Liz let out a shriek. "Congratulations!"

"Oh, my gosh!" I screamed and ran to the car. Lizzie scrambled out, and we hugged and jumped. "I can't believe it!"

"Believe, believe! If you believe in fairies, clap your hands!"

"Hold it." I stopped. "What if . . . yeah . . . I bet Sarah tried out for Peter after I left. This sign isn't meant for me."

Lizzie looked crestfallen.

"This sign better *not* be for me. I could never do it."

The door opened and Dad stood grinning. "Well? Did

I, or did I not, tell you this morning that you're good? That ol' gusto did it again. Congratulations, Peter."

"Dad, are you sure you got the message right? *I* got the lead? What about Sarah?"

"She's Mrs. Darling. She doesn't know yet, though. I'm leaving now to pick her up at the mall."

"Wow, I can't believe it. Oh, gosh—the lines. Think of all the lines. What if I can't learn them all?"

"Don't worry, Chris," Lizzie said. "You can do it. I'll help."

"Liz," her mother called, leaning across the car seat, "we'd better get home now. Congratulations, Christy. Be sure to save us tickets for the show."

As I walked into the house, Mom was coming up from the cellar with a bag of dog food under her arm. Beezer was right behind her. As Mom squeezed me, the bag slid down my leg and thudded to the floor. "Chris, you must have been terrific this morning. George said you were the unanimous choice. You had such spirit."

"He said that? Really? Are you sure he didn't say I had *too* much spirit? And Mom, what about all those lines?"

"You can handle it. You don't have to learn all the lines at once, you know. You do it gradually."

"And what about Sarah? Will she be okay about getting the part of Mrs. Darling and not Wendy?"

"It's a good role for her. I think she'll be happier with it in the end."

When Sarah walked in, she congratulated me, then went straight to her room to get ready to baby-sit.

"Well," Sarah said as she joined us later at the dinner table, "having no figure has some advantages."

"Sarah," Mom said, looking annoyed.

"Just kidding."

Kidding or not, she got me thinking. Maybe my spirit wasn't why I got the part.

I excused myself as soon as possible and went up to my room. Below I heard Sarah saying, "I *said* I was kidding. But really, her audition was embarrassing. Enthusiasm is one thing; she got carried away. And you've gotta admit, she hasn't exactly 'bloomed' early. I'm sure that looking like a boy helped her get that part."

"Sarah, your attitude needs improving," Mom commented.

"And when you get to like your own part more, you'll feel better about Christy's," Dad added.

"I would rather be Wendy," Sarah admitted, "or some fun part. If people outside the family didn't consider me so mature and proper, maybe I could have gotten a more fun part."

I got off my bed and closed my door. I hoped that Sarah was wrong about the reason for my getting the part of Peter.

"Hazel, are you a late bloomer, too?"

Five

Monday morning felt unfriendly. Getting up might be a mistake. I lay still and tried to ignore the morning noises the rest of the family was making. The chances that someone would roll out the red carpet for me at school because I had the starring role in a play were slim. The chances that someone would make a crack about my audition were fat.

Topics for our science projects were due today. I was topic-less.

Old locker number 66 was probably still thinking it was protecting the crown jewels.

I stared at Hazel and sighed. She stared back.

"Up and at 'em, Christy!" Dad bellowed.

"Rats." I pushed my blue quilt to the end of the bed with my feet. White jeans and a blue shirt were hanging over the desk chair, all ready. They looked too cheery, but I didn't feel like putting together a different outfit. What I wore seemed like the least of my worries.

Choco Crispies. Precisely the cereal to feed a lost cause. No sense wasting Mom's homemade granola. "That's no way to start a good day," Mom said, as I poured the cereal into my bowl.

"It isn't going to be a good day," I mumbled.

"Hmmmm?"

I didn't answer. I just mashed the Choco Crispies against the roof of my mouth with my tongue.

Dad was packing our lunches while Mom poured juice and doled out vitamin pills. "Here's an extra iron pill, Christy. You look like you could use a boost. It's a bit early in the year to be dragging." Mom looked at me closely, then reached across the table and felt my forehead. "You don't seem to have a fever." She looked hard at my Choco Crispies. "I wish people would stop bringing junk food into this house."

Dad winked at me as he spread cream cheese on rye bread.

I was sorry I didn't have a fever. If I'd known things would be this awful in middle school, I'd have tried to stay back. Even my sister seemed to like me better in the old days. Peter Pan never had it like this.

As I got up from the table, I stepped on Beezer. That's the only way I knew she was there, she's so quiet. One of my jobs is to give Beezer her heartworm pill in the morning. I shoved it into a glob of cream cheese and held it over her head. She looked up, ready for me to drop it into her mouth. I let go. It landed on top of her head and stuck to her fur. She looked ridiculous as she looked around for the cheese, with it sitting on her head.

Sarah began to laugh. "Jeez, you're a clutz, Beeze."

"Some of us aren't perfect," I said.

"You're telling me," she muttered under her breath.

I wiped off Beezer's head and went upstairs to finish getting ready. "Prepare to meet thy doom," I said to myself, feeling like one of Captain Hook's prisoners about to walk the plank.

The abominable locker was ready for me. It had been planning its strategy all weekend. I knew it. Ready with my counterattack, I fished down into my overstuffed bookbag (I was afraid to put much in my locker, in case I never got it out of there again), and I pulled out a can of 3-in-One oil. I'd seen Dad squirt it on every lock, motor, and wheel on our property and I figured it couldn't hurt. When the oil began trickling down my locker door, I decided I'd used enough.

Next, I gave the locker a kick with my sneaker to show who was in charge. Then, I pulled my backup weapon out of my bag. I'd brought along a hammer.

Right 25 . . . "Ya better," left 16 . . . "open up," right 4 . . . "or ELSE," PULL . . . "you're gonna get it this time."

I was waving the hammer when Lizzie stopped next to me. "Chris, what are you doing? Yuck—your locker is all greasy."

I shook the hammer at the locker, then began to bang the lock.

"You can't do that! That's vandalism, Christy!" Lizzie screamed. A small crowd of kids gathered around us.

I felt like one of those people threatening to leap from the top of a tall building with people below yelling,

"JUMP!" I clutched the hammer and stood there. Anger and embarrassment flooded over me. I couldn't think what to do next. Finally I handed my weapon to Lizzie. "Hold this."

Right 25 . . . left 16 . . . right 4 . . . click. Click? CLICK! I lifted the locker handle and bowed. Mild applause from the crowd. They wandered off, looking disappointed that I hadn't done something really violent and had to be dragged off by the authorities.

"Wow, Chris, you're certainly starting the day off dramatically. Stardom has quite an effect on you," Lizzie said.

"Very funny. Now I've got to find my vocabulary book. It has to be somewhere in this idiotic locker." I poked around the bottom of the locker, pushing things from side to side. There was a brown lunch bag squashed against the back. As I picked it up, a greenish furry thing fell out. "Oh, yuck."

"What's that?" Lizzie asked, her nose wrinkled in disgust.

"It was once part of a lunch."

"Ick. Is it some new health snack of your mom's?"

"Don't be gross. That's mold." I flicked it out onto the hall floor. "Sorry, Mr. Johnson," I said as I thought of him coming down the hall with his broom and arriving face to furry face with that foul thing.

Gym was first period. At least my gym locker caused me no real problem. The lock was a removable combination padlock like the one for my bike.

I changed quickly into my gym clothes. Spending more time than necessary undressed when one is built like Peter Pan is downright foolish. In health class the teacher said that each person develops at his or her own individual rate. My rate must be snail's pace.

Lizzie and I trotted outside. In shorts, Lizzie's legs looked longer and thinner than ever, and as we jogged around the field, she reminded me of a colt.

"I don't have a science-project topic yet," I said.

"You don't? You *have* to have one today."

"I know, but I don't. I can't think of anything."

"I'm doing something with batteries and bells. It was my father's idea," Lizzie said. Her father would be more help than mine.

We jogged silently for a minute. I was hoping the fresh air and oxygen would give my brain a boost.

"Don't you think Todd is cute?" Lizzie asked.

"Who?"

"Todd. Over there. The Todd in our science class. The same Todd I told you about last year. The only boy in the seventh grade who's a decent height."

"Oh. Sorry." I was panting now. "I keep forgetting that now that we're in the same school," pant, "all the kids we've been telling each other about all these years," puff, "are all here." I looked over to where Lizzie had pointed. "Yeah, he is pretty cute."

We finished our laps and flopped to the ground on the side of the field where Ms. Bolen and Mr. Norden call roll.

"Todd is a friend of Jeff's, you know," Lizzie went on, breathing hard. "I've seen him at the Matthews' house a few times. He came with Jeff to deliver the newspapers one time. Naturally, I looked disgusting that day."

"I wish Jeff were in another class of mine besides science. But I'm glad he's not in this class. I'd rather he didn't see my knobby knees . . . and banged-up shins . . . and wilted hair after I sweat . . ."

"ALL RIGHT! Listen UP!" shouted Ms. Bolen, giving her whistle a sharp blast for emphasis.

"Allen?"

"Here."

"Barton? Uh, Barton, where are your white socks? We don't wear pink in this class. Understand? That's a check mark for you."

I looked down to be sure my socks were white.

"Braun?"

"Here."

"Downey?"

"Here."

"Downey, don't stand too close to anyone today. Those gym clothes of yours never made it home for the weekend, did they? I can tell whose clothes went home to be washed and whose sat in a smelly heap all weekend. A check mark, Downey."

Downey's face turned red. Maybe Downey had as much trouble with locks as I did.

"Listen up, now. We're playing flag football today."

Several kids, mostly girls, groaned.

"You moaners, pipe down. This game will benefit some of you who don't know what's happening on a football field. I know some of you are cheerleaders and don't have the foggiest idea when to cheer. Correct?"

Behind me I heard Beth Roman, who's been cheering from the time her twin brother was a "midget peewee" player. "I *hate* football. I couldn't care less what they're doing on the field."

"Me too," her friend whispered back. "I cheer 'cause I like cheering. And I love the outfits. Football I can't stand."

It was difficult following what Ms. Bolen was saying. She rattled on quickly about rules and positions and grabbing flags off players' belts. She spoke as if we already knew it all. I glanced around to see if anyone else looked confused. I tried to hear what Mr. Norden was saying as he gave directions to the other half of the group. But the wind was carrying his voice the other way.

With Jeff's friend, Todd, in the class, I wasn't about to sound dumb by asking questions. I'd just fake it and do what everyone else was doing.

Ms. Bolen named one captain, and Mr. Norden chose the other. Todd was one; the other I didn't know. I kicked at a clump of grass along the sideline until somewhere in the middle of the choosing I was picked by the kid I didn't know. He obviously didn't know me either—I felt anonymous.

The captains handed out the flags and belts. I waited a minute before doing anything. I wanted to be sure I knew what I was supposed to do. It was easy. One end of the flag just got stuck into a belt, and the rest of the flag dangled.

Positions were assigned. "Where?" I asked when I was told mine.

"Over there," my captain said, pointing.

I nodded and trotted over to where he had pointed.

Unfortunately, Lizzie was way across the field on Todd's team. She was the only one I'd have asked about this game, which I was beginning to hate already.

Ms. Bolen stood on one side of the field, and Mr. Norden stood on the other. A whistle began the game. Todd kicked off and some heavy guy on my team caught the ball and ran. Kids began charging this way and that. It looked to me as if our runner needed help. Poor guy—he was being attacked from all directions, and no one else on my team was even trying to rescue him. What an awful game. I didn't know what I was supposed to do, except that the flags had a lot to do with it all. Not wanting to look like a complete dud who didn't care, and wanting to make it clear that not choosing me right away was about as dumb a mistake as any captain could make, I decided to make my move. I swooped and darted, grabbing as many flags as I could.

"Look at her!" someone screamed.

Exhilarated, I hurtled on, dodging and snatching. My arms were overflowing, flags were flapping behind me.

"Oh, jeez, whose team's she on?" someone asked.

A whistle blasted three times and I stopped.

"Swan, I've never seen anything like that," said Ms. Bolen shaking her head.

"Thank you," I answered modestly. Giggles rippled through the class. I looked around. Lizzie had her hand over her eyes and was staring at the ground. My face began to burn and my stomach tensed.

"Swan, ONLY the ballcarrier's flag is pulled off. It's done instead of tackling, don't you see? You can't just run around and grab everyone's flag. Understand?" Ms. Bolen said. "By the way, are you Sarah Swan's sister?"

I nodded.

"Amazing."

I managed to get through the rest of the game. Humiliation settles me right down. So does having teachers ask me if I'm Sarah's sister.

Mr. Norden was nice though. He winked at me when I was over on his side of the field, and he said, "I like your team spirit and aggressiveness. It's important in sports." At least he hadn't decided I was a total ding-a-ling.

In the locker room, I said to Lizzie, "Oh, God, I hope Todd doesn't tell Jeff. Do you think he will?"

"Hey, Christy," Beth Roman called across the room, "that was some play you made. From what I heard about your audition, I guess you really throw yourself into things, don't you?" She chuckled.

Liz bristled before I had a chance to answer. "Oh, yeah? Well, she got the lead, for your information."

Beth looked surprised. She had no answer for a change.

Lizzie slumped to the bench, looking glum. "That shut her up." She kicked off a sneaker. "Do you know that when Todd picked me on his team he actually said he didn't know my last name?"

I waited. There would be more.

"Can you believe that? Can you? For the last year and a half, I've known his first name, middle name, and last name, as well as his address, *and* his phone number! I even know the names of his sisters and what kinds of cars the family has." Lizzie looked both discouraged and outraged.

"*And*," she went on, getting up, pacing, and waving

her hand in the air, "did you notice how much attention he paid Michelle Ferris? How could any boy be seriously interested in a girl who arrives at school flat-chested, goes into the girls' room, then comes out two minutes later with big boobs? She's the only kid I know who wears four socks a day instead of two."

I had to laugh.

"I'm stupid to like Todd. He has no taste."

"Well, he probably just needs time. When he gets to know you better, things could change. Too bad he didn't see you tell off Beth. You were great. Thanks."

We finished getting dressed in silence. As we were gathering up our books, I said, "I feel as though a time bomb is ticking. In three hours and twenty-two minutes we have science."

Six

By the time science class rolled around, I was panicking. I looked around the room at all the eager faces waiting to impress Mr. Abbot. Blank. That's all I had—a blank brain.

"Well, people, I am anxious to hear what you have decided to do for your projects. As I read down the class list and call each name, please tell me your ideas."

"Todd." Mr. Abbot smiled expectantly.

"Uh, I'd like to study the menamortic . . . no, wait . . . melimofic . . . whatever—of a caterpillar."

"Metamorphosis?" Mr. Abbot offered.

"Yeah, that's the word. I think I'll study a few different types of caterpillars and compare them at different stages."

"Sounds fine. All right, Andy?" Mr. Abbot continued down the list. My stomach was doing triple flips. My brain was spinning but getting nowhere. Being toward the end of the alphabet was giving me time, but it wouldn't have mattered if my last name were Zilch. I was still blank.

"Lizzie."

Lizzie matter-of-factly described her bells and batteries idea. Behind her, Jeff looked calm as he waited. He must have felt me looking at him because he turned and smiled. What a perfect smile—straight teeth, slight dimple, sparkly eyes. Wow. Why did it have to be only in science that he saw me? Why not reading, or English, or music?

"Beth . . ."

Oh, help. Mr. Abbot was down to Beth Roman. A cold, sick feeling washed over me. I was going to have to say something. *Any*thing. I didn't hear what Beth said, nor Eric Sutton. I just knew Swan was coming up.

"Well, Christy, I see you made it on time today." He smiled but he probably didn't mean it. Most likely he was getting pleasure out of embarrassing me. "All right, what will your project be?" My mind was racing, but words weren't coming. "You haven't left your ideas locked in that famous locker of yours?"

I squirmed. It would have been better if *I* were in that locker, mold and all . . . mold . . . hey!

"Mold." I blurted out.

"Mold, Ms. Swan?" he said, looking puzzled.

"Yes, all sorts of mold. I'm going to grow and study mold." I smiled and sat up straight as various members of the class expressed their disgust.

"Interesting. Unusual. Hasn't been done as long as I've taught this course. Mold has possibilities." Mr. Abbot sounded pleased.

I felt about one hundred and sixty pounds lighter with Mr. Abbot off my back. Maybe things were starting to look up.

"Michael Taylor."

Silence.

"Project please, Mr. Taylor."

Silence.

I looked at Michael sitting next to me. Taylor. So that was his last name. He was staring at his desk. But he did flex a grubby sneaker a couple of times, indicating that there was some life in him.

Mr. Abbot began to rap his pencil against his clipboard. He walked closer. His suit smelled like stale pipe tobacco. "Surely you have a project, Mr. Taylor. Forty percent of your grade depends on it, you remember."

Flex.

Mr. Abbot's face tightened. He rapped faster.

My God, I thought. That could have been me Mr. Abbot was glaring at. Think, Michael. Come on, think! I wished my brain were bubbling over with topic ideas—and I wished I could launch one into the air over to Michael. But this was science, not science fiction.

"I shall be forced to deduct points if you do not come to me with your topic by the end of the day. Understood?"

Michael raised his eyes and looked at Mr. Abbot's angry face. "Yes."

"By the end of the school day," Mr. Abbot repeated.

I saw a look in Michael's eyes, as if he put miles between himself and the rest of us. I was more interested in that than in mold, but felt pretty sure Mr. Abbot wasn't in the mood for a topic change at this point.

* * *

"Let's go."

"What?"

"Come on." Lizzie stood next to my desk, books in her arms and purse dangling only inches from my nose. Most of the other kids were already out the door or headed for it. Mr. Abbot was filing papers in his desk drawer. Class had ended without my having noticed.

"Okay," I said, looking to see if Jeff had left. I caught a glimpse of what looked like the back of his head. The backs of most boys' heads look pretty much the same, but I could pick Jeff's out of a crowd. His was perfect.

"Liz," I whispered, as I gathered my books and got up, "what do you think of Michael?"

"He's not off to much of a start. I mean, it's not *that* hard to come up with a topic."

I shot her a look.

"Oh. Sorry. But you did, at least, come up with something at the last minute. He should have just said anything for now. He could always change his mind later."

"I feel sorry for him. He seems to be having a lot of trouble," I said. "I wonder what's wrong?"

"Oh-oh. Here we go. If I know you, you're about to get involved. Think it over, Chris, he's weird."

"But he looks so—"

"Chris," Lizzie interrupted, "not another stray, please."

"What?"

"Stray. As in that huge black dog you took in once."

"That was ages ago. Besides, the owners finally showed up," I said, stepping to one side to avoid being rammed by an eighth grader.

"And, as in that hurt bunny you tried to nurse back to health, but couldn't."

"Yeah, but—"

"Wait—I'm not done. Remember that baby squirrel that fell out of the tree? And you tried to help it . . . then it bit you and you had to go get a shot?" Lizzie looked at me sternly.

"Well, this is certainly not the same sort—"

"Chris," Lizzie said, cutting me short again, "all I'm saying is think about it."

I did . . . and I thought Michael might need a friend.

Seven

I knew very little about mold except that it grew nicely in my locker. Mr. Abbot said we had to turn in a written description of our proposed topic by Wednesday, and it was obvious I'd have to do some fast research. The eager-beaver students would have cleaned the school library out of the good science books, but there wasn't much danger of the mold books being gone. They'd probably been sitting for ages, gathering mold. If not, I'd call Mom and ask her to bring home a few things for me. She's a librarian at the state library and can get just about any book I need.

I stopped in the library after my last class. Standing at the card catalog, flipping through cards, I froze. Jeff and Todd walked in. Did I want them to see me or not? That was quickly settled. They headed straight toward me.

"Hi," Jeff said.

"Hi," I squeaked back.

"You getting your science stuff?" Todd asked.

"Uh-huh."

"You really going to study mold?" Todd wrinkled his nose at the thought.

"Yeah, I think so. I had to pick something, and that just popped into my head."

Jeff chuckled. Maybe that was a good sign. At least he didn't act revolted by my topic.

I didn't know what I should do next so I jotted down a couple of Dewey Decimal numbers and said, "Well, I'll see you." I found the science section and a couple of mold books. Lingering between the stacks, I peered through the books on the shelves and watched Jeff and Todd talking by the card catalog. Stupidly, I stayed where I was until they left.

Trudging home, I thought of how Sarah would have handled things. She'd probably have managed to get a movie and a pizza out of that one brief encounter.

Sarah was standing at the door as I came up the front walk. "Hurry up. We have our first play practice today."

"I know that, but I had to go to the library."

"Well, move it. You can't act like a prima donna around here," Sarah said.

"A what?"

"A prima donna. You know, the female lead. But the type that keeps people waiting and is a pain to work with," Sarah explained, checking her hair in the hall mirror.

"All I did was stop at the library. Besides, we don't have to be there until four, and it doesn't take me hours to get ready, like someone around here," I grumbled, letting the screen door bang.

"Hi, Chris, how was your day?" Dad asked. He was

coming down the stairs from his study. From the wrinkles in his pants, I could tell that he had been writing at his desk.

"Okay. I conquered my locker and chose a science project."

"Congratulations on both. What did you decide to study?"

"Mold."

"Hmmmm." Dad always says that when he's trying not to sound as if he has an opinion. "What led you to choose mold?"

"It's a long story. My locker helped me with the decision."

"Sounds intriguing. Someday you'll explain, I hope."

"Get ready, Chris. Charles and Stanley will be here any minute," Sarah called.

"Who?"

"Two boys from the play called to ask for rides," Dad explained, "and Sarah said it was fine before I had a chance to tell her that today isn't the best day for extra passengers."

"Why? What's today?"

"Beezer has to go to the vet for her shots this afternoon. Since the theater is so close to the clinic, I'm taking her at the same time I take you."

A person would have to have ridden in the car with Beezer to understand the situation. Just the mention of "car" makes her so nervous she starts slobbering and trembling. That's only the beginning.

The doorbell rang and Sarah cheerfully invited Charles and Stanley into the living room. The door triggered the cookie connection in Sarah.

"Want a cookie?" she asked. Charles' round shape made it clear that he seldom turned down an offer of food.

"Sure," he answered enthusiastically.

"No, thanks," said Stanley, who was half the width of Charles.

Charles' broad hand scraped the bottom of the cookie jar. I thought of a bear scooping a great glob of honey.

"What part are you?" Stanley asked, seeming to have only just noticed I was there.

"Peter."

"No kidding. Really?" He looked at me with raised eyebrows and new respect.

"That was some audition," Charles mumbled, spitting crumbs as he spoke.

"It certainly was," commented Sarah.

Dad jangled his keys as he walked into the room. "Everybody ready? Someone get Beeze on her leash while I lock the back door."

Standing beside Dad's VW, we must have looked like one of those clown acts where they all stuff into one tiny car. They don't include one carsick dog though—one that absolutely has to sit up front, or ELSE. We squished in, Stanley on top of Charles, me sitting on Sarah. Beezer wouldn't get in, even with Dad tugging on her leash from inside. So I had to pry myself out and push Beezer from behind.

Finally we were all in. As we chugged off, Sarah started giggling about how funny it all was. Dad turned and gave her a look which quieted her right down. There are times when his patience and good humor get strained, and with Beezer drooling all over the gearshift and onto his khaki pants, this was one of those times.

"Well, Mr. Swan," Charles said, somewhat muffled from being under Stanley, "we seem to be making it without disaster."

Just as Charles finished speaking, Beezer heaved the contents of her stomach all over Dad's shoe.

"YUCK!" Sarah said, opening the window and sticking her head out. I gagged and put my head out too.

"Argghh," Stanley said. "Are we almost there?"

Dad had barely let the car come to a full stop in front of the theater before we opened the door and scrambled out, still holding our noses. "'Bye, Dad," I called as he drove off. I'd seen him look happier.

As we walked toward the door, Sarah poked my shoulder. "Don't play up the star bit, Christy."

Most actors and actresses really try to get into their roles, and "become" the characters they play. How was I supposed to be the most humble, modest girl alive, while playing the part of a cocky, conceited boy? I'd have a split personality before the play was over.

Until now I'd always felt secure in knowing that what I did or didn't do wasn't going to make or break the play. Being the lead would be no picnic. There was a lot of responsibility.

After George went over our practice schedule, we read through a couple of scenes and did a few songs. The choreographer explained some of the dance numbers.

"When can we begin rehearsing the pirate scenes?" Charles asked, eager to throw himself into the role of Smee, Captain Hook's first mate.

"We'll start later in the week," George said. "For now, I want you all to read, and reread, the play. Think about your characters, start learning your lines. Any questions? Okay, see you Wednesday."

As we gathered our things to leave, I saw someone come in the side door and head toward the piano. It was Michael Taylor.

What was he doing at the theater again?

I slid into a back-row seat to find out.

"Okay, I guess you're the first one here," George said. "I'm sorry we ran late last Saturday. Thanks for coming back. Let's get started. Your name is—"

"Michael Taylor."

"How long have you been playing, Michael?"

"Seven years."

"And you've studied with?"

"My grandfather."

"All right. Why don't you play a couple of things you know, then I'll give you some music from the show and you can try that," George said.

Michael began. I knew the song he was playing; it was "Maple Leaf Rag." We had it on a Scott Joplin record. I checked his fingers to be sure he was really playing. He was so good, so light. It looked easy for him. His next song was a classical one which I'd heard before but never thought anyone my age could play.

Out of the corner of my eye I caught Sarah waving at me, mouthing, "Come on." I got up slowly and quietly walked out.

"Christy, you could have been out here five minutes ago," grumbled Sarah. "Prima donna."

With no Beezer and no extra passengers, the ride home was a lot easier than the ride to practice had been.

The car still smelled though, so we rode with all the windows down.

"What took you so long, Chris?" Sarah asked.

"Someone I sort of know was auditioning for accompanist. I couldn't believe it."

"Why not?" Dad asked.

"It was amazing. He was so incredible, so terrific. But in school he's a miserable zero."

"Hmmmm."

"I can't explain how different he just was. It was as if he were another person."

"Who is he, anyway?" Sarah asked.

"Michael Taylor."

"Don't know him."

"You're not the only one," I said.

"Taylor. Hmmm," Dad said. "It's a pretty common name, but you never know. . . ." Dad's voice kind of trailed off.

"Never know what?"

"Well, it's doubtful that it's the same family, but there used to be a Taylor who lived in town who was quite a musician. He played with some of the great old jazz bands." Dad paused, then added, "In fact, he may even be on one or two of my old albums."

"Hey, that must be the same family then, Dad. Michael told George that his grandfather taught him."

"Could just be a coincidence," Dad said.

"Leave it to Christy; she'll find out," Sarah said.

I didn't answer. Sarah leaned forward and switched on the radio.

Dad whistled and drove.

I stuck my head out the window and thought.

Eight

Peter Pan had a point. Things like school and growing up get complicated sometimes. A simple thing like going to the girls' room can turn into a fiasco. On Tuesday after math I got stuck in a stall. Two of the coolest girls in the entire school came in and stood by the sinks doing their hair and makeup, while I was silently trying to get the stall door open. The bell rang. They didn't leave. They just kept on spraying their hair and glossing their lips. Cool kids never rush. I did, though. Feeling like a complete fool, I crawled under the door. Keeping my head down, I rinsed my hands and ran. "Who was that, anyway?" one of them said. Sniggers and cackles trailed after me as I dashed down the hall. Last year it would have been funny.

Lizzie had a rough day, too. Using all her courage, she gave Todd a candy bar with her phone number written inside on the foil. It was a simple enough idea. The problem was that he broke it in half, foil and all, and gave the half with the phone number to another kid. Now the wrong boy, worse yet, a very short, chunky one with a fat, blurry voice and a crush on Lizzie, has her number. That, too, would have been funny last year.

At dinner that night Sarah said, "Mom, you have to do something about Chris."

"Such as what?" she replied, looking at me curiously.

"Tell her to wear a bra."

"A bra? She doesn't need one yet," Mom answered.

"Well, you haven't really noticed her then. I have—at rehearsal today when she was strutting around crowing. It was embarrassing."

"For whom?" Mom asked.

"Me!" snapped Sarah.

"You're being silly, Sarah."

I sat like a lump as they talked around me, as if I weren't there. Some of our dinner conversations are better (or worse) than others, but this one hit a new low. I glanced at Dad to see if he looked uncomfortable. He was leaning to one side and glancing at the newspaper lying on the floor by his chair.

"I have an old, one-size-fits-all bra I'll give her. She has to wear something," Sarah, the authority, continued.

No, I did not.

"It's up to Christy. There's really no rush," Mom answered.

"Thank you, Mom," I mumbled.

"There is too a rush, Mom. Do you think there are other girls in middle school who don't wear a bra? She's not in Neverland." More unasked-for comments from Sarah.

"A girl named Margaret Barton in my gym class just got her first bra. I don't think her family was scrambling to get her into one," I snapped. "She's already a C."

"A C-what?" Sarah said.

"At least a C-plus!"

"Oh, God, Christy—you're so dumb! I mean, thirty-C, thirty-two-C, thirty-four-C, what?"

"How should I know? I'm not as interested in bras as you obviously are."

Later that night I found an old, wrinkled, stretched, grayish, one-size-fits-all lying on my bed. I tossed it in the corner. No way would I wear that ugly thing.

After all, I'd been cast as a boy. That says something. But, on the other hand, I didn't want to be a little kid forever. I certainly didn't want Jeff to think of me as that. I guess what I wanted was not to be pushed by Sarah.

I succeeded in ignoring her complaints for a couple of days, then finally I picked up the atrocious thing and tried it on. It felt odd, sort of like an undershirt that wasn't pulled all the way down. I didn't like it. But I left it on anyway, carefully covering it up with a dark-green shirt that no one could see through. I checked the mirror to be sure the straps and back part weren't lumpy enough to be noticed.

Friday night, after another rehearsal, Sarah complained again. "I don't know which is worse—Christy with no bra, or Christy singing 'I Won't Grow Up' while tugging and yanking on one! Mom, can't you do something?"

My face was hot. Sarah was giving no thought to how

embarrassing this was for me. I couldn't even fit into a supposed one-size-fits-all. Why wasn't I one of the 'all'?

"I am getting irked, with a capital U," I said.

"A what?" asked Sarah.

"A capital U!"

"You can't spell, dummy."

"Okay then, a capital E."

"Wrong again." Sarah was laughing. Mom was trying not to.

"All right. I'm getting damn mad. How's that!"

"Chris, you have a right to be annoyed," Mom said. "I know you could do without Sarah's advice on this subject. If you have decided to go ahead with the bra business, which should be entirely your decision, I'll get you a couple of new ones which won't be so tired and stretched out."

"Okay," I said, getting up to leave. "I have to go read about mold now."

"Hey, Sarah," I yelled later that night as I lay on my bed surrounded by science books, "did you know that at this very moment you have mold floating around you? It's in your shoes, and it's even all over your gorgeous hair!"

"Christy, that's totally revolting!"

"Watch out, Sarah. Rhizopus nigricans is coming to get you . . . and even YOU cannot escape." Cackle, cackle.

I liked the fact that practically perfect people are covered with mold.

Nine

Michael walked into play practice Monday afternoon. I hadn't seen him in school for a while. I wondered if he was avoiding science, or was sick, or if there was another reason. It had been a week since auditions and he hadn't shown up at rehearsals either. But I knew he'd be our accompanist. No one else could have auditioned that well.

The piano bench squeaked against the floor as Michael pulled it under him and sat down. He began to play quietly as people milled about before practice started. Gradually the cast became still. Kids stared at Michael. Lightly he played song after song, from memory. George set aside his clipboard and got up from his seat. "Kids, this is our accompanist, Michael Taylor."

Michael nodded, barely looking up.

"I see what you mean," Sarah whispered. "He's good."

"He hasn't been around for days. Wouldn't you think

he was supposed to be?" I said, pulling my rolled-up script out of my jacket pocket.

Sarah shrugged. "Don't know."

Rehearsal was fun. Having the piano made a big difference. Michael played so easily, barely looking at the music, and he seemed to know just how to do each song. He played them exactly the way George wanted.

Michael looked different than he did in school. With the piano in front of him, he seemed comfortable. At one point I was sure I saw him smile as he was playing one of Captain Hook's numbers while Stanley and Charles clowned on stage. It was the best rehearsal we'd had. A lot of the credit had to go to Michael.

I wondered if he recognized me from science class. I was a lot bolder in the theater, as Peter Pan, and even as myself. Some of Peter's personality must have been rubbing off on me. Probably Michael didn't notice who I was, since he never seemed to look at anybody in school.

When rehearsal ended, I went to the back of the theater to find my jacket. George walked to where Michael was gathering up his music. I was sure he'd say something about Michael's missing rehearsals.

"Nice playing, Mike," George said. "How'd everything go last week?"

"Tough."

"I can imagine. Did Justus understand why he had to go, do you think?"

"I'm not sure. Maybe. I think so," Michael said.

I felt like an eavesdropper—I *was* being an eavesdropper actually—but I didn't know how to leave without making it obvious that I'd been right there and had heard what they were saying.

"How are things at your aunt and uncle's?" George asked.

"Okay."

"I'm glad, and welcome to the theater group." George jumped onto the stage and closed the curtain.

As I walked out with my jacket, I smiled in Michael's direction. His head was down, so I couldn't tell if he saw me. I wondered what he meant when he told George that something had been tough last week. Whatever it was, George knew about it and let Michael miss a lot of practices because of it.

"Dad," I said later that night, "will you try to find those records that might have Michael Taylor's grandfather on them?"

Dad looked up from his book. "It may take some time to dig out those old albums, but I'll see what I can do."

"Want some help?"

"No, thanks." Dad went into the den and rummaged through his collection for several minutes. Then he called, "Here they are. My old cockeyed filing system isn't half bad." Dad grinned and held up two albums.

I looked on the back of one where the musicians were listed. Justus Taylor—Piano. "That's the name, Dad. I heard Michael say something about Justus today. That's him."

"Let's put one of these on," Dad suggested. The piano playing on the record sounded a lot like Michael's. I recognized one of the songs—he'd played it, in the same style, before rehearsal started.

"Dad, what do you think has become of Justus Taylor?"

"I have no idea."

The phone rang. "Chris, it's for you," Mom called.

"Hello?"

"Hi, Chris. I have to tell you this," Lizzie said. "Jeff has some science books I need."

"Yeah?"

"And I'm going to have to borrow them. Want to come?"

"Hold it. How do you know what science books he has?"

"Dad was talking to him today when Jeff came with the newspaper. They got onto the subject of the science projects and Dad found out about them. Now, do you want to come?"

"Right now?"

"The sooner the better. The books I have don't help me at all," Liz said.

"I doubt if I can go—we're about to have dinner—but I'll see. Hang on."

Mom's answer was exactly what I expected. "It's too close to supper," I repeated to Lizzie. "Are you really going?" I asked.

"Ummm . . . guess not—not without you. This is a good chance for you to see Jeff. I'll wait till you can go," Liz answered.

"Maybe you should just do it. I'd be scared anyway. I get petrified talking to him in school—no way would I dare march up to his front door. I'd probably end up crouched in a bush."

Liz laughed. "If you want him to notice you, you can't go around hiding in bushes."

"Okay, I'll work on boosting my bravery level. Maybe

we can go tomorrow. Hey, you know what? Michael Taylor played the piano at rehearsal today. You wouldn't believe how good he is."

"Really? He seems like such a zero."

"Well, his grandfather was a famous piano player. We even have some of his records."

"That's amazing," Lizzie said. "No one in school would guess any of that."

"Certainly not Mr. Abbot," I said.

"Especially not him," laughed Lizzie. "I can't believe Michael hasn't given Mr. Abbot a topic yet."

"I know. I'd be so scared to show up in class."

"Doesn't he know he's got to do some, *any*, sort of project—at least to keep Mr. Abbot content?"

"You'd think so. But Michael's different. He doesn't even act like the same person at rehearsal that he is at school. He's really involved at rehearsal—seems happy almost."

"That's a switch."

"Chris, dinner," Mom called.

"Okay," I answered. "Gotta go. I'll talk to you tomorrow."

I thought some more about Michael—it was true that no one in school would ever suspect Michael came from a talented family and was a better musician now than any of the rest of us could ever hope to become. It might be nice for him if they knew. Probably a lot of people would be impressed—not just kids, but teachers, too . . . maybe even Mr. Abbot.

Ten

When we walked into science the next day, a substitute was standing at the front of the room. She looked young. By the grins and signals, it was clear the class decided she couldn't be too experienced.

Everyone was slow to settle down. Finally the substitute cleared her voice and screeched, "I'm Miss Wilcox and I'm going to take attendance."

Then it got awfully quiet.

"Thank you." She looked a little surprised at how suddenly we stopped talking. "Margaret Barton?"

"Here."

"Todd Chander?"

"Here," Andy said, giving a cheery smile.

"Andy Haskell?"

"Here," Todd answered. I could see his shoulders shaking and knew he was trying not to laugh.

On down the list.

It caught on fast. Beth became Amy, I became Lizzie, and so on. Someone became Jeff, and when Miss Wilcox reached Michael's name, Jeff answered. Michael looked up at Jeff, who was grinning at him. For the first time all year, Michael kept his head up, partway anyway. Maybe with Mr. Abbot out, he felt braver. And maybe what Jeff did helped.

"Now," Miss Wilcox said, "as I went down that list I noticed the name Chander. I have a history class at the college this semester with a Professor Chander."

Andy glanced at Todd, who gave a tiny nod. "Yep, that's my dad," Andy said.

"What a coincidence," she replied.

"Uh, how's his dad as a teacher? Is he good?" Todd asked.

"Very good, but tough. You look a little like your father, Todd," she said to Andy.

"Really?" Andy said.

"How 'bout me, Miss Wilcox? Do I look like his dad, too?" Todd asked.

She looked puzzled, then answered. "As a matter of fact, you *do* look like him. Are you two related or something?"

Muffled giggles. I glanced at Michael and saw him smile, which was a first in this class.

"Okay, kids, let's get started. The lesson plans say that there's homework to be corrected. Get it out and exchange papers."

There was a flurry of papers as they went from person to person, finally ending up back where they began. Jeff was busy copying over his homework. Why was he doing that? Then I saw him whisper to Todd to hand it to Michael.

As the papers were corrected and the grades called out to Miss Wilcox, I saw that Michael was part of the class for once. He wasn't actually fooling around or volunteering, but he did look at the paper and correct it.

I decided to give talking to Michael a try. "Michael," I whispered, "you are a terrific piano player. Rehearsal was so good yesterday."

He turned to me, said nothing for a minute—probably just noticing for the first time that I was in the play—then he nodded and turned back to the paper on his desk.

I figured that was it for the conversation, but he surprised me. "Your part takes a lot of energy—and you've got it," he said.

I took that as a compliment. "Thanks."

"Keep it up," he said.

Aye-aye, Captain, I thought. I decided a weird conversation was better than none—and he seemed to be trying to be nice.

We were given time to begin the next chapter. I was just starting when the intercom startled me. *"May I have your attention, please. Liz Manning report to the office, Liz Manning to the office."*

Lizzie gasped but didn't move. No one did. Miss Wilcox waited for Liz Manning to get up and leave. Would she remember which person answered to that name? "Go ahead, Liz," said Beth, looking directly at me. I glanced quickly at Liz, who gave me a helpless shrug. Twenty-three grinning faces watched me stand up and weave my way between desks. The strap of Andy's backpack looped on my foot and I had to shake it off.

Once outside the door, I tried to be calm and plan my next move. Maybe it wouldn't matter if I wasn't really Liz. Maybe they hadn't called her for anything important. But what if they had? I took a couple of steps in the direction of the office, then stopped outside the girls' bathroom. I could hide. Eventually they'd forget about wanting to see Liz. But Ms. Bolen came striding down the hall, whistle swinging across her chest. "Do you have a hall pass, Swan?"

"I was called to the office." That was sort of true.

"Hustle then! You're wasting class time standing here."

"I'm going," I answered. If I didn't go, the class would never let me hear the end of it. What was the penalty for impersonating another student?

I took a deep breath as I rounded the corner and faced the glass wall of the office. There by the counter was Liz's mom, holding Liz's trumpet.

"Hi, Mrs. Manning. Liz is in the bathroom, but I'll take her instrument to her. Thanks." Snatch. I hardly gave her a chance to answer. Trumpet in hand, I hurried back to class.

The homework assignment was on the board. Some of the kids were writing it down, while others were leaving. Michael was already by the door. I held up the trumpet and tried to look as if it had been no big deal passing myself off as another student. Grins and thumbs-up signs made the whole thing seem worthwhile.

Out of the corner of my eye I saw Jeff coming toward

me. "That must have been some tense trip to the office," he said, smiling.

"Yeah," I answered. "Luckily it was only Liz's mom there."

"Good thing. How's the mold growing?" he asked.

"Fine, I think. Some types are taking a while to get going, though." I wondered if they give lessons in small talk anywhere. I'd sign up in a flash if they did. Making sure Michael had left before I spoke, I said, "Why'd you do your homework over and give the extra copy to Michael?"

Jeff hesitated for a moment. "Aww, I don't know. Just an impulse. School doesn't seem to be his thing. I sit near him in history and he's pretty much tuned out there, too. And yesterday I walked behind him on my way to soccer practice. You wouldn't believe where he lives. It's falling apart."

"His clothes are a mess," commented Lizzie, who'd just joined us.

"I heard him say something yesterday at play practice about an aunt and uncle. You'd think they'd noticed how he looks. The shirt he had on today was torn and had a button off. The only place he seems to look better is at rehearsal—guess he cares more about that."

I started to explain about the play, but Lizzie cut me off, which was just as well, anyway. Jeff would probably never fall for a girl who played the part of a boy.

"Yikes! Look at the time!" Liz said as she looked up at the clock. The three of us hurried out the door.

"See you," Jeff called as he headed toward the gym.

"Chris, you must have been petrified going to the office," Lizzie said.

"You're right. I was. Now that it's over, though, it's pretty funny. Actually, if I can convince people I'm Peter Pan, I should be able to impersonate you."

"Peter Pan was shorter, don't forget," Lizzie said, laughing.

Teachers were beginning to close classroom doors, and the bell for the next class was about to ring, so we walked faster.

"That was really nice of Jeff to make Michael feel a part of things today," I commented. "Did you notice him doing that?"

"Yeah. He's a pretty nice guy," Lizzie said. "Smart, too."

"Seems like he does well in science—does he always do well?" I asked.

"All the times I've been in classes with him, he has. He and his brother are both pretty serious students. Their dad is some sort of dean at a college and has them go to special Saturday classes for really smart kids."

"Oh, yuck," I said. "I don't think I'd go for that."

"I don't know whether Jeff does or not, but his family puts a lot of pressure on him."

"It sounds horrible—six days of school. Five is plenty," I said, reaching for the door to reading class. Especially of middle school, I thought to myself.

Eleven

I'd seen some pretty interesting mold lately. Some types just conveniently showed up around the house, and others I had to grow on purpose. Mom keeps a couple of empty coffee cans by the kitchen sink and we toss organic leftovers in them for the compost pile. I photographed a spiky fuzz-ball with black nubs on the tips of each spike growing in one of those cans. The back of the refrigerator also turned out to be a haven for forgotten items.

"Oh, my gawd!" Sarah screamed last night as she stuck her fingers into a dish tucked in the corner of a kitchen cupboard. She'd been feeling around for snacks. "What in . . . oh, jeez." She ran to the sink and squirted dishwashing detergent on her hand. Rubbing furiously, she yelled, "Chris, what's the disgusting crud growing in that dish in the cupboard?"

"Huh?"

"You heard me!" Sarah twisted the faucet off hard and grabbed a towel. "Mom, she shouldn't be allowed to grow mold in our kitchen cupboards. I'm calling the Board of Health if she doesn't stop."

"Chris," Mom said, "what exactly *do* you have growing up there?"

"It's just an old peach. Mold grows faster in dark places, so I put the peach in a dish and stuck it back there. I didn't think anyone would touch it. If Sarah wasn't always looking for food, she wouldn't have."

"Well, I think you should clear your mold-growing spots with the rest of us before you leave any more around."

"Okay." I picked up my camera and snapped a picture of the peach, which looked like a furry green tennis ball, then I tossed it out. I tried to snap a picture of Sarah too, but she wouldn't let me.

I had other types of mold growing in secret places around the house, but I didn't think this was the time to go into detail. Mom was already repulsed by my slime mold which was creeping around the old fish tank in my bedroom. She asked me to move it to the garage or throw it out.

As I probed further into my topic, I was developing new respect for mold. It's very determined stuff. If it doesn't have just the right conditions, such as water, air, and food, it doesn't give up and die—it just WAITS. It can wait for years and years. That's kind of creepy really; I can picture the sinister spores just lurking, biding their time. . . .

That got me thinking—about conditions, about being determined, about biding time, and about Michael.

I was glad we had a day off from school, thanks to a Jewish holiday. I needed time to work on the written part of the report. The public library was the best place to go because I never have much luck working on major school-projects at home. Distracting myself is so easy. Things such as Sarah's nail polish or old letters in my desk can take on new interest.

I called Lizzie and we arranged to meet at the library at eleven. We meant business and agreed to take our lunches so we couldn't leave when we were hungry.

I jammed my books, papers, note cards, pens, pictures, and lunch into my backpack, told Mom where I was going, and peddled off on my bike. It was a clear, crisp morning, too nice to be inside all day. I was glad we'd at least be having a picnic lunch.

The library was rectangular, with an adult section at one end and a kids' section at the other. I hesitated for a moment, then headed for a table in the reference area of the kids' section. I was just putting my information on Roquefort and Camembert cheese molds into piles when I saw Lizzie coming through the heavy front door. Behind her, someone had a leg out, holding the door open. Jeff was attached to the leg.

As soon as Lizzie reached my table, I whispered, "What's Jeff doing here?" I could feel my face beginning to burn.

"Dad and I were driving along our road and we saw him walking this way. So we stopped and offered him a ride. He's working on his project too—only he's further along than we are," Lizzie said as she dumped her books and papers onto the table. Between the two of us, we covered the entire table with our stuff. "He gave me the books I need, so that's good. Now you won't have to crouch in any bushes."

"I'd love a bush right now. I look awful." I said. Out of the corner of my eye I could see Jeff looking for a place to work. He ended up two tables away. I didn't know how I'd ever be able to concentrate with him right there. And I thought it would be distracting working at home!

"Hi," he said, giving me a smile as he pulled a sheet of paper from his notebook.

I smiled back. "Lizzie, this won't work," I whispered.

"What won't?"

"I won't. I can't work with Jeff two tables away. My chest is thumping, my hands are sweating, my retainer is in—"

"Then why don't you go to the ladies' room and take your retainer out if it bothers you?" Lizzie suggested as she tried to find room for her long legs under the table. "I wish they'd put a few taller tables down at this end," she muttered. "Maybe it's time to graduate to the adult section."

"I'd have to walk across the whole room to get to the bathroom. Can't you block me while I spit it into my backpack?"

"Okay," said Lizzie, who had to shift way over to one side after having finally gotten her legs settled.

With my foot, I pulled my backpack next to me. "Okay," I whispered, "lean over." As she moved in front of me, I gave my retainer a nudge with my tongue and it dropped. Both Lizzie and I gasped as it bounced off the side of the backpack, hit the table leg, and rolled out onto the floor.

"Ohhh, nooo," I said softly, staring at the retainer lying in plain sight on the floor.

"Relax," Lizzie said.

I looked up and saw Jeff walking into the adult wing. I kept my eyes on him as I reached for the retainer. What a great walk he had. And absolutely nobody else's jeans fit that perfectly.

My supposedly serious workday was turning into something else. Mold was definitely becoming a second-class interest. Concentrating on my project was difficult, but I really wanted to get some work done and out of the way. There was a limit to how much of my life I was willing to devote to mold and Old Frogface.

Lizzie worked busily. I concentrated on concentrating. After a while, Lizzie poked me, offering a lemon drop. "Did you know," I whispered, "that there's mold in those drops?"

"Oh, come on."

"I swear. Wait a minute. I'll show you." I burrowed down into my backpack and finally held up an index card. "It says that Aspergillus mold is used to make citric acid, which is what makes the flavor sour." I gave a satisfied smirk as I leaned back and waited for Lizzie to react.

"Ohhh YUCK!"

"Yuck what?" said a voice next to me, which made me jump. A voice that sent lightning bolts into my stomach. I hadn't seen Jeff come back into the room.

"Yuck to what Christy just said. She told me these lemon drops have mold in them."

"Seriously? You kidding?" Jeff asked.

"She's not."

I swallowed hard before trying to speak. "Lemon has citric acid in it, and when citric acid is made in a factory, black Aspergillus mold is used to make it." I felt almost breathless after that. Talking to boys wasn't as easy as Sarah made it look.

"I don't think I can enjoy these now," said Liz, still holding the box. "You want one, Jeff?" She held up the box.

"Sure. Mold's been in them all these years, I doubt it'll make me sick now, just 'cause I know it's there." Jeff grinned his fabulous grin, then added, "You know, you have a pretty interesting topic."

"Yeah, it is, I guess. But I'm not a natural-born scientist, that's for sure."

"Most people aren't," Jeff answered. As he leaned on the table, I noticed the nicest veins running down his arms.

Lizzie's stomach rumbled. "Let's go outside and eat," she suggested, pushing back her chair. "You're welcome to share," she said to Jeff.

"Thanks. I'm going to finish one more thing. Then I'll come out."

"What'd you bring?" Lizzie asked as we pushed out through the heavy doors.

"Nothing too exciting. Tomato and cheese on whole wheat, apple, and a root beer." We headed toward a big stone bench under some trees, off to the side of the library. "I don't know if I can eat with Jeff around."

Liz unpacked her lunch onto the space between us on the bench. I held my bag unopened on my lap.

"Jeff is the best-looking guy I've ever seen, Liz. I wish I were less like me and more like Sarah right now."

I heard the library door open and knew Jeff was walking our way. "Did someone offer food?" he said.

"Yup. Have a Fig Newton." Lizzie held up the bag with one hand and reached for her orange soda with the other. Jeff caught my eye and grinned as he looked at the soda. I knew what he was thinking.

"Uh, Liz, you don't want that soda, do you?" he said.

"Of course."

"Mold and all?" he asked.

"What mold? Oh, good grief, not again." She looked at her soda. Jeff nodded. "More citric acid? More Asper . . . Aspergunk?"

"Aspergillus. 'Fraid so," I answered.

"Let's have all the bad news at once. What else do I have that's mold enriched?"

"Well, let's see," I said, smiling. "You'd better check the bread for penicillium. And those potato chips—watch out for potato blight. Those cookies could have wheat rust. . . ." Lizzie looked pitiful. I'd ruined her lunch for her.

"Hmmm, what are you willing to give up now?" Jeff asked.

"Take your pick," Lizzie answered, scowling.

"I had some pet fish once which were eaten alive by some mold growing on them," Jeff said calmly, as he crunched one of Lizzie's chips.

"That's IT! *NO* more! For the rest of the day, not one more word about m-o-l-d. Got it?" Lizzie sounded definite.

"Okay. How's your project coming along?" I asked Jeff. I noticed that he had really nice hands.

"Not bad. I don't have much more to do. Aren't you going to eat?"

"I might have something in a while. Do you want something?"

"No, thanks."

"Speaking of projects, come on. We better all get back to work. Chances are Mr. Abbot will be back in school tomorrow," Lizzie said. "When he checks our progress, I, for one, want to have some."

We worked all afternoon. My progress was divided. Some in the area of mold, the rest in the area of the person sitting two tables away. He was a serious worker, I could see that. But when he'd look up and catch me watching him, he'd smile or whisper something funny. I decided he was about the most perfect boy I'd ever known.

Twelve

Sure enough, Mr. Abbot was back the next day. When I walked in and saw him, I quickly looked to see if Michael was there. He was.

The period began as usual. Mr. Abbot told us to take out our homework. We started going over it.

"Michael, number seven," said Mr. Abbot. "What were some of the problems Louis Pasteur faced as a scientist?"

Michael looked up but didn't answer. His book lay closed in front of him. I glanced at Jeff and knew he was wishing it were today he'd given a copy of his homework to Michael, instead of when Miss Wilcox was substituting. Lizzie chewed her thumbnail and stared at her paper. Time seemed to have stopped.

"The answer is right in the book, Mr. Taylor. I suggest you open it," Mr. Abbot snapped, coming so close I could smell his frogbreath.

Michael flipped through the book once, without really looking at the pages. "You, Michael, are going to fail this class. I suggest you buckle down." Mr. Abbot strode over to his desk, picked up his clipboard, and ran his finger quickly down his paper, as if he were checking. I knew he didn't have to check. "Your project topic has never been given me, Mr. Taylor. Call home after class and explain that you'll be late this afternoon." Mr. Abbot seemed to be almost snarling through his pipestained teeth.

Uh-oh. There went rehearsal. We'd have no accompanist. And Michael would miss out on doing something, maybe the only thing, he really seemed to enjoy. If he'd just do *some* sort of project and *some* homework, a small attempt, things would be okay. What was the matter with him anyway?

Without Michael's music, that afternoon's rehearsal was sort of a dud. George persuaded one of the stage crew to play some of the numbers, but it wasn't the same. We ended up concentrating on the scenes where we didn't need the piano as much.

"Kids, before you leave, I want to hand out these new practice schedules. A few times and dates have been changed, and I've added a couple of extra rehearsals in October, as we get closer to the performance date. Be sure to let your parents know the changes."

"You have a practice listed on Columbus Day, George, but we don't have school and some people might be away," Stanley pointed out.

"Yeah, I know. But for those who'll be around I'd like a rehearsal. This could be one of the best productions this old Forum Theater's ever seen. The more time we put in, the more top-notch it will be. And, by the way," George added, "I have to say that Sir James Matthew Barrie, who wrote this play, would be proud of you all if he could see how well you're doing."

We all cheered and slapped each other on the back.

"Okay. See you all tomorrow," George said. "Oh, wait—does anyone see Michael Taylor? I want to be sure he gets the new schedule."

I figured I could give it to Michael in school tomorrow so I raised my hand.

Wrong. The next day Michael was absent.

"Lizzie, I have to get the new play rehearsal schedule to Michael, but he's not here and I don't know where he lives," I said when it was clear Michael wasn't going to show up for science. Mr. Abbot was ignoring us while he filed papers from the class that had just left the room.

"Hmmm. Didn't Jeff say he saw where Michael lives?"

Pound, thump. Pound, thump. The thought of asking Jeff had a horrible effect on my heart.

Lizzie leaned across the aisle. "Psssst. Jeff. Where does Michael live?"

Jeff looked puzzled. "What?"

"Chris needs to know where Michael Taylor lives."

"Ah-*HEM*," Mr. Abbot cleared his throat. "Take out today's assignment, please."

Jeff mouthed, "Tell you later."

Knowing that Lizzie and I would be talking to Jeff after class made me nervous the whole period. My voice squeaked when I was called on for an answer.

Each time I looked over at Jeff, he seemed to be frowning a bit. When the bell rang and Mr. Abbot dismissed us, I asked Liz if she noticed how Jeff looked. She said maybe he was jealous that I was asking where Michael lived. I was just starting to think about that when Jeff walked over to where Liz and I were waiting. Pound, thump.

"You want to know Michael's address?" Jeff asked.

"I have to take him something," I said.

"Oh . . . Well . . . you go down South Avenue to Meade Street, then cut across the baseball field to Locust Street . . . you look confused. Do you know where I mean?"

"Not exactly, but I'll find it. Go on," I answered.

"After you pass the old Baptist Church on Locust Street, look for an old, run-down, brown house on the left. I don't know the number, but it's the most run-down one on the street."

"Okay. I think I'll find it," I answered.

"Wait a minute. I have soccer practice after school anyway. The field's over that way. Meet me at the front door by the buses after school. I'll show you the house."

Lizzie winked.

I pounded and thumped.

Thirteen

Tingly terror. That's what I felt the rest of the day. Sir James M. Barrie wouldn't be too impressed if he saw the chickenhearted side of me. Peter Pan had spunk, but full-time spunk is hard to sustain. Even mold takes time off when conditions aren't good.

I got to the front door of the school before Jeff. He came along with Todd a minute later. "See you," he said to Todd as they reached the door. Todd looked puzzled, then smiled when he saw Jeff come up to me and say, "All set?"

"Are you bringing Michael his assignments?" Jeff asked as we walked down South Avenue.

"No, it's a rehearsal schedule. He's the piano accompanist for the play I'm in. The director asked me to give it to him." I glanced at Jeff—did he look relieved that this was not a social visit to Michael's? I couldn't tell.

"Oh, yeah. You said something about rehearsals. What's the play?"

I hesitated before answering. *"Peter Pan."*

"I saw that in New York a few years ago. It must be a fun play to do."

"It is," I said, smiling.

"What part are you?"

"Peter."

"Hey, you must be good! Congratulations." He didn't give me a weird look or say anything about my having a boy's part. Relief.

After we crossed the baseball field and turned onto Locust Street, my arms started to ache from all my books. I shifted my load.

"Want me to carry some of those?" Jeff asked.

"I'm fine, thanks."

"I have half as many as you."

"I know, but that's my fault," I said, laughing. "I still don't trust my locker enough to leave anything important in it."

Jeff reached over and took two books from my stack. Again, I couldn't help noticing the great veins in his arms. Something must be seriously wrong with me. It's normal to notice a person's eyes, or smile, or build . . . but veins?

I'd never seen Locust Street before. It was unusual. One house had small plaster trolls and a "Beware of Dog" sign on the front yard. Across the street another house had fake ducks and a deer. Further down the street were two Virgin Mary shrines, one with a fountain, the other with spotlights.

We walked by the church. Even that didn't feel friendly. Then Jeff slowed down as we approached a brown house. "This is the place," he said. "But it doesn't look as if anyone's home."

From the condition of the driveway, it didn't look as if anyone had been there in quite a while. It was overgrown. There was a rotting front porch with vines growing on it. They looked like poison ivy.

"I'll go up and ring the bell," I said. "Thanks for showing me where the house is."

"You're welcome, but I'm waiting until you're done."

"You'll be late for soccer practice."

"That's okay."

I climbed the worn steps to the door and pushed the doorbell. No answer. It didn't sound as if the bell worked. I tried knocking. Still no answer. "You're right. Nobody's here."

Then I heard a noise. "Ooops, I take that back. Maybe someone is here," I said.

"We can try around back," Jeff suggested. We banged on the back door, carefully, because one of the windowpanes was cracked. "Let's look in." Shielding our eyes with our hands, we could see into the kitchen. Two empty peanut butter jars, a soup can, and an open pack of Oreos lay on the counter. Unwashed dishes were on the table and in the sink. Hanging over a chair were a dirty sweatshirt and a worn-looking flannel shirt. On the floor, some in a bowl and some not, was unfinished cat food.

"I must have heard a cat," I said.

"Hey, there's some mold for your project," Jeff remarked. "I wonder who's in charge of cleanup here? Whoever it is, is doing a cruddy job."

We wandered around the side, but bushes kept us away from windows. "There are windows in the front. Let's look . . . no, maybe we shouldn't—the neighbors might call the police on us," I said.

We looked anyway. Through one front window we could see into a room that was probably supposed to be a dining room. But there was no dining room furniture, only two pianos piled high with music. Some postcards were tacked on the wall.

"That's interesting," I said. "Someone sure likes postcards, but no one seems interested in the newspaper." I stepped over several days' worth of papers lying on the porch.

Jeff had moved to the other front window. "Here's the living room," he said. I looked in and saw a television with some photographs on top. Nearby were a dilapidated couch and chair, and a vinyl-covered footstool. A few more postcards were propped up next to the photographs. A boy's jacket was lying on the couch, and two soda cans and a bag of pretzels were on the floor.

"Well, I guess I'll just stick this schedule in the front door and hope it doesn't blow away. Or do you think I should try to stuff it in this mailbox?"

Jeff was frowning. "Jeff?" I said.

"This is pretty interesting," he said.

"What is?"

"Well, think about what you saw inside. What kind of food was left around?"

"Nothing fancy, that's for sure. Stuff that would really make my mother cringe."

"Clothes?"

"Kids'."

"Does it look to you as if a car's been in and out of this driveway lately?"

I looked at the grass growing up through the cracks in the tar. "No," I said turning to Jeff.

"Who do you think's living here?" he asked.

"Looks like maybe no adults—but from what I overheard him say before, it sounded like he's staying with an aunt and uncle. So don't you think he could just be coming by here to feed the cats?"

"Maybe, or maybe he is really living here . . . all by himself. . . ."

Fourteen

Over the weekend I thought a lot about Jeff and what he and I had seen. When I told Hazel about it, she gave me that look . . . the one that means, "Here you go again—be careful." She's kind of an inner voice that tells me to slow down sometimes. But I don't always listen.

I also told Lizzie about it, and she said, "You don't really know for sure, though."

"No—not for sure, so I guess I'd better mind my own business until I know what's going on. But if there's a chance he's alone. . . . Lizzie, don't you know how scary that would be? All alone?"

"Yes, but you don't really know anything definite yet. It could be embarrassing for a lot of people if you poked into a situation that doesn't need poking into."

"True, but I think we should 'probe further,' as Mr. Abbot would say," I said. "A responsible person would."

"Maybe, but remember—this is real life, not a Nancy Drew mystery. Be careful."

We left it at that.

When Jeff was absent from school on Monday, I felt crummy and let down. The more I got to know him, the more I liked him.

Michael wasn't absent, however, and I almost wished he were, to avoid another detention. Our play needed him more than Old Frogface did.

It was a hot, sticky, Indian summer day, and several of the science-room windows were open. I looked at the treetops to see if I could see any breeze moving them. Nothing. Even up here on the second floor there was nothing. It was very uncomfortable.

Before class started, kids were talking and fooling around. I was about to ask Michael if he got the schedule I'd left for him when Mr. Abbot told everyone to sit down and get out the homework. As we went over the assigned questions, I noticed how limp my paper felt from the weather.

When Mr. Abbot called on Michael and got no answer, I could feel the tension in the room. Something, or somebody, had to give.

"I'm waiting for the answer to number nine, Michael."

Silence.

"You're holding up the class," Mr. Abbot said through clenched teeth.

Silence.

I wished Michael would just say *some*thing. He didn't have to make things this bad. Why did he, anyway?

"It will be another detention for you, Mr. Taylor. And I'm phoning your parents directly after class. Have you anything to say about that?"

Silence. Then Michael shifted in his seat. All eyes were on him. Looking down at his desk rather than at Mr. Abbot, he cleared his throat, then said, "No one's home."

"Well then, I'll try until someone is. I'm sure they'll be interested in your progress—or lack of, I should say."

I felt myself squirming. I didn't see how Michael could stand the pressure he was creating. There had to be a reason he was allowing this to happen. A small effort could have avoided it; he must have known that.

Mr. Abbot's face glistened with perspiration. He must have been really hot in his brown suit. Its stale smell was stronger than ever. Todd rolled his eyes and wrinkled his nose when Mr. Abbot moved closer to Michael and stood next to Todd's desk.

"Michael, students just don't ignore my assignments. Do you understand? Your parents must be made aware of the situation." Mr. Abbot fingered the pen in his hand. "And perhaps a good shake-up is just what you need." He turned and walked to the blackboard. Michael mumbled something under his breath, but I couldn't hear what.

Mr. Abbot began to talk about atoms, which we read about for homework. He took some colored chalk out of his desk and started drawing atoms on the board, making protons, neutrons, and electrons different colors.

As Mr. Abbot was involved in his drawing, Michael gathered up his few books, stood up, and quietly left the room. I looked at Lizzie in disbelief. She was as shocked as I was. Never in a hundred years would either of us dare to walk out of a class.

Several boys looked at each other and grinned.

A few minutes passed as Mr. Abbot continued about atoms, erasing parts of some and adding them to others. As he kept talking about how elements and molecules are made, it started to make sense.

Mr. Abbot was engrossed in his blackboard atoms and seemed unaware of the restlessness behind him. Subtle signaling and whispering went unnoticed. Then he turned to ask a question. "Which one of these atoms has a plus charge? Remember, count the . . ." His voice trailed off. He looked bewildered for a moment as he looked around the room at the uneasy faces. "Uh . . . count the . . ." Then his eyes fixed on Michael's empty seat.

I shifted in my chair and looked at the blackboard. Maybe if I could quickly answer the question—I started to add up the protons, hoping they were the right thing to count.

"Where is Michael?" Mr. Abbot asked.

I stopped counting.

No one said anything. I glanced at Lizzie, who stared frozen-faced at a corner of the blackboard. Except for Beth Roman pulling at a cuticle, and Eric cracking his knuckles, the room was still.

Mr. Abbot's eyes scanned each row, as if he somehow thought Michael would appear in another seat. "Michael . . . what's happened to him?" Mr. Abbot looked from face to face. His eyes finally rested on Todd. "Todd?"

"Uh—I think he had to go somewhere," Todd answered.

"Had to go somewhere?" Mr. Abbot clenched his jaw and fingered a piece of chalk in his hand. "Not without a pass. Students don't leave without a pass," he mumbled to himself as he looked at us, or rather over us.

A long moment later he collected himself and said, "Stay in your seats, please." Then he left.

No one moved.

Shortly after, we all heard the intercom blare. "*Michael Taylor to the office. Michael Taylor to the office immediately.*"

Neither Michael nor Mr. Abbot returned to class for the rest of the period.

Fifteen

Word spread quickly through the school about what happened in science. Everyone was sure Michael would be suspended. I doubted that would happen right away, and I was right. Neither Michael's parents nor a guardian could be reached. That I learned from a girl who was waiting for the nurse when the secretary was trying to reach the Taylor family. Michael was temporarily assigned to the detention lunch-table. He was also assigned daily visits to the guidance counselor.

I had just gotten home from school when the phone rang. Since so many calls are for Sarah, I let her answer.

"For you," Sarah said, dropping the receiver on the counter. "Sounds like a boy."

Pound, thump. "Hello?"

"Hi, it's Jeff. I was absent today and wonder if we have any science homework."

"Are you sick?"

Jeff laughed. "You mean because I was absent? Or because I seem so eager to get the homework?"

"Yes . . . either one."

"I'm not really sick. This morning I felt rotten, but now I'm not too bad. My brother had a twenty-four hour thing on Friday and I guess I caught it."

"I'm glad you're better. You really missed something today." I told him what had happened in science and mentioned that no one could be reached at the Taylors'.

"That doesn't necessarily mean much. No one would be home in lots of houses," Jeff said.

"True. But at least the office has other numbers where parents can be reached. He must not have turned any in."

"You're probably right. That's kind of strange, Christy, don't you think?"

"Yeah, it is. And what he did in class . . . well, I was worried about Mr. Abbot for a while there. He looked awfully upset."

"That was pretty extreme, walking out," Jeff said.

"You know, Mr. Abbot isn't really all that bad. Michael's been asking for it from him. The rest of us have been treated okay," I said. "I mean, I admit Mr. Abbot can seem scary, but if you do your work and try in class, he's all right."

"True. Actually, he can be pretty funny," Jeff said. "Yesterday my Spanish teacher had an emergency and had to leave. Mr. Abbot filled in for him and was joking around. He didn't know much Spanish so he made up words and tried to fool everyone. It was a good class."

"I wonder if . . . maybe, for some reason . . . Michael's trying to get attention. I don't know if that would make sense, though. But nothing about him seems to make sense," I said.

"He's hard to figure," Jeff said.

"For sure. Well, anyway, with all that went on today we didn't get a homework assignment. I guess we could just wait until tomorrow and see what he wants us to do."

"Sounds good. Okay, thanks a lot. See you tomorrow," Jeff said.

I smiled . . . twice. Once, thinking about seeing him tomorrow, and once more because he called *me* for the assignment. There were plenty of other people he could have called.

We had rehearsal that afternoon and Michael was late. It seemed to take him a while to get into the music, but once he did, we had a super practice. Things were starting to come together—the music, dancing, sets, costumes, and best of all, the group spirit. We were all having fun. Even Michael laughed when the girl playing Tinker Bell missed her cue to come into the Darlings' nursery. She couldn't open the window and ended up kicking it in, which was hardly the delicate behavior of a fairy. The light, tinkling piano notes that Michael normally played to accompany Tinker Bell's flutterings became loud, thunderous chords as she attacked the window. Everyone broke up.

When it quieted down, George said, "Remember, Tinker Bell, you have a role normally played by a flashlight. Go easy on the bashing and crashing." He winked at her.

After rehearsal ended and everyone was leaving, George came up to me and said, "Christy, you see Michael in school, don't you?"

"Uh-huh—in one class."

"Is everything okay? He seems kind of unsettled and has missed some rehearsals. Is anything wrong, do you know?"

I fiddled with my jacket zipper. "Well . . . he's been getting into some trouble in school." I felt like a tattletale, but George did ask, and maybe he could help.

George hesitated, as though he didn't want to say too much. "Michael doesn't exactly have an easy home life . . ."

"I know that. I went to where he lives, on Locust Street, to give him the new schedule and—"

"Wait a minute," George broke in. "Michael doesn't live there anymore. He's with relatives."

I stopped zipping. "Oh, good. It sort of looked as though someone was still living there when I stopped by with the schedule, and I was pretty sure he got it. Maybe he just stops in to check on things."

"Probably. He used to live there with his grandfather, but Justus broke his hip a while back and Michael had to help him settle into a convalescent center. That's why he missed rehearsals in the beginning. Now he's staying with an aunt and uncle."

"Okay, that's good. Maybe they'll help him."

"Help him with what?" George asked.

"With science, for one thing. He could get suspended for something he did today."

"Chris, can *you* help him?"

"Me? I don't know. I don't really know what the problem is. He hardly ever talks to any of us. But I could try."

"Fine. We'll both work on it. I feel I owe it to Justus. He's a good man and was one heck of a performer. And Michael has his talent."

After dinner I said, "I don't have much homework. I think I'll take Beezer for a walk." Happy thumping from under the table seconded the idea.

I always feel safe walking with Beezer at night. Even though she's the most wimpy-hearted thing on four legs, she's big. People don't mess with big dogs.

I headed in the direction of Michael's house. I wanted to check it again. "Dummy, do you know what you're getting into? Of course not, but you'll do it anyway," I said to myself.

Beeze had to stop and sniff every telephone pole, bush, tree, and curb along the way. She saw no connection between the "heel" command learned in dog obedience class, where she'd been a star, and the "heel" command given in the outside world. She was snuffling along with such concentration near the corner of Runyon Avenue that she walked into a tree.

I was relieved when we finally reached the baseball field. There were fewer things to slow Beezer down, and I was able to get her to lope across to Locust Street.

It was beginning to get dark but people were still outside. An elderly man sat smoking a cigarette on the front steps of the house with the plaster trolls. A heavy, dark-skinned woman was washing her car in the driveway next to the fountain Virgin Mary shrine. Beezer growled at a cat crouched under a truck parked in front of the church.

I slowed down as we neared the Taylor house. A light was on inside. I wanted to get close and look in, but with the neighbors outside, that didn't seem like a good idea. I tried to think of an excuse to knock on the door. Something to do with the play—but Michael had just been to rehearsal, and anything important would have been said then. School, homework . . . no. Slowly I walked by the house and on to the end of the block. Pulling Beezer around, I turned and walked back. While I kept my eyes on the house, I let Beezer stop and sniff the overgrown bushes and weeds by the Taylors' driveway.

I was looking at the peeling paint when a shape passed in front of the window. I strained my eyes to make out who it was. It was hard to be sure. I glanced around to see if anyone was watching me. The man with the yardful of trolls had gone inside, but the car washer was still out. She was more interested in her hubcaps than in me, though.

The back door of the house banged, and moments later a cat scampered into some high grass along the side of the house. Beezer never saw the cat, she was so busy checking out the ground smells.

The car washer was drying off the car and had her back to me, so I took a few steps toward the house and stared at the windows. I caught a glimpse of movement.

Then came the piano music . . . it was from *Peter Pan*. Michael had to be in there. The question was . . . was he just stopping by . . . or staying over?

Sixteen

Mr. Abbot's junior scientists continued to plug along on their projects. That is, all but one. Michael visited the guidance office during science period.

My many molds were progressing nicely. I made little signs saying, "*DANGER*—mold experiment in progress," and taped them around the house. I even taped one of the signs on my locker door. A trace of my original mold had remained in the locker, and until I had positively identified and photographed it, I had to protect it.

"My batteries and bells are really starting to get to me," Lizzie said. "I'm hearing ring-a-lings in my sleep. It'll be nice when this is over."

"Yeah," I said, as we walked from English to music, "but Sarah says we'll have to do bugs next."

"Argh."

We passed the gym. It was empty except for two long ropes hanging from the ceiling. I stopped by the door. Grinning, I said, "What do you think? Should we?"

"Love to, but I can't. Not in this skirt," Lizzie answered.

"Looks all clear. I can't resist. Hold these, will you?" I gave Lizzie my books. "One, two, three . . ." I raced across the gym, grabbed a rope, hitched up my knees, and swung high off the floor. If only George could rig up wiring, I could do this in the play. I burst into my "I'm flying" song.

A mistake.

My super soaring was suddenly interrupted by two sharp blasts of a whistle. Ms. Bolen was standing in the locker-room doorway.

"Get down *right* now!" she ordered.

Easier said than done. Stopping gracefully, or even quickly, wasn't easy.

One angry lecture and one class period later, I found myself at the detention lunch-table. Teachers are allowed to give either lunch detentions or after-school ones, or both. At least I didn't get both.

"You'll never believe whose sister *that* is," I heard one kid say.

"What's Christy doing at the prisoners' table?" asked another. I could feel the stares.

I tried to look nonchalant despite my humiliation. There weren't too many of us at the long table, but the others looked like hard-core delinquents. They were probably regulars with season seats. I chose a spot way down at the opposite end from the others.

A minute later Michael arrived. He hesitated a moment. "Here," I said, pointing to the spot across from me. "Have a seat."

He sat down and silently unpacked his lunch—a peanut butter sandwich, chips, Oreos, and a soda. Not a lunch my mom would approve of. And maybe not a lunch an aunt or uncle would go for either. I guessed that the cookies were soft and stale from sitting out. They looked like the ones I'd seen from his kitchen window. If they were, then he *must* be staying at the house. He must have spent the night and made the sandwich in the morning. It was almost proof.

I wasn't sure how to begin, but I knew I had a chance to do what I'd promised George I'd try. "It's good you have this detention instead of the after-school one," I said.

"Hmmm."

"It would be terrible if we lost you as our accompanist. You're terrific."

"Thanks." He took a bite of his sandwich.

Conversations where the other person gives one-syllable answers are frustrating. "I guess you got the new rehearsal schedule."

"Yup."

"I left it at your house."

"Thanks."

"After I told George I left it there, he said you probably wouldn't get it. He said you'd moved."

Michael stopped chewing. He was silent for a moment. Then he said, "I got it when I went to check the house."

"And feed the cats?" On impulse I decided to risk

saying that to see what he'd do. Even though cats can be left alone, maybe if he knew that I'd seen the house that closely, he might admit that he was still living there, if he was.

"What?" He paused, then said, "Yeah, that too."

That didn't tell me much. But I'm not a quitter. "So, are you out of science now?"

"Not really."

"But you're never in class anymore," I said.

"That's just this week. I have to see the guidance person, shrink, whatever."

"What about the project?"

He shrugged. "I haven't been too organized lately."

"Don't you have to do one?"

"Guess so . . . eventually." He reached for his soda and took a drink.

Boy, I thought, he certainly had a knack for being casual. It was ridiculous that I was more worried about his project than he was. But I had promised George I'd try to help, and besides, I couldn't put my finger on it, but there was something about Michael that made me want to help. Maybe I just didn't want to see a guy with such talent go to waste. "Couldn't you do a project that has something to do with music?" I asked.

"That doesn't sound like science."

"Sure. You could connect music to science somehow." I tried to sound enthusiastic. My mind raced, trying to think of a connection. "Ah-ha! Remember Pavlov's dogs? It was in one of our chapters. He used a bell to get the dogs to respond. You could do something with piano tunes, or chords, and your cats."

"What?" He sounded only mildly interested.

"Maybe one line of music or one chord could be a signal that you're going to feed them. Another signal could be for playing with them. Another could be for when you're going to let them out." I smiled, impressed with my own fast thinking. "What do you think?"

"I don't know. Maybe," he said, crumpling up his lunch bag.

"Or, maybe," I said, feeling on a roll with good ideas, "you could do something with vibration and strings. You know, catgut—*not* from your cats, of course." Where were all these good ideas when I needed them before?

The first bell rang, letting us know we had five minutes to finish up and clear out. I realized I hadn't eaten. Quickly I bolted down my chicken sandwich and gulped my juice. "See you at practice," I said to Michael as I hurried out of the cafeteria.

Lizzie was waiting for me. "Wow, no one could believe you had lunch detention. That was some group at the table."

"Sure was. I had a talk with Michael."

"Yeah, I saw. What'd he say?"

"Well, not a lot. But maybe, just maybe, I've given him an idea for a science project. And I really think he's living alone."

"Did he say that?"

"No, not right out, but I'm pretty sure I'm right."

"You're going to tell now, aren't you?"

"I don't feel I can yet. There must be a good reason he's doing what he is . . . that is, if he really is doing it."

"Uh-huh." Lizzie looked very thoughtful.

"Well, I think he is. And I also think that *he* knows that *I* know. I can't rat on him yet. If he trusts me, I can help him more. At the moment though, I'm not sure if he wants help or needs help. It's hard to tell."

"I certainly think he'd need it. I get scared just being in the house alone for a short while. Imagine what it's like for him," said Liz.

"I know. I think about it a lot. Plus, think of all the things adults do to run a house. If he's there alone, he must do all that himself . . . how would he even know how?"

Sarah was waiting for me on the corner after school. That didn't happen often these days. "I hear you got busted today. You know what Ms. Bolen said to me in the hall?"

"What?" I cringed at what was coming.

"She said, 'Boy, Sarah, your sister is nothing like you. She's so impetuous.'"

"Oh," I said.

"That really ticked me off."

"Oh," I said again. I didn't know what impetuous meant. I doubted it was something good.

Sarah kicked a pine cone into the gutter. "She had no right to discuss your problems with me and compare us." Another pine cone went flying. I wasn't sure what Sarah was complaining about. She must have come up looking pretty good in the comparison.

"She's stupid," Sarah went on. "Does she think I'm perfect? I don't want a goody-goody reputation." Kick. "It's borrrrring."

"I never knew you felt like that." I was really shocked. It had never occurred to me that Sarah might not like her image.

"Now you know. Maybe, just maybe, you'll hear about me getting into trouble next week." Sarah smirked.

"You're kidding."

Giggling, Sarah explained how she and a friend had talked about working out a plan with their math teacher to have it look as though they were getting into trouble. They were both sick of being predictably polite.

"What are you thinking of doing?" I was amazed by the whole thing.

"We might ask Mrs. Williams if she would announce that absolutely no one is allowed to go for a drink during next week's quiz. Then right after she finishes saying that, we'll get up and ask for a drink. She could act furious and tell us to sit down."

"Yeah? Oh, my gosh."

"Then we could walk right out to the drinking fountain while she yells and pretends to be mad at us. That would shake up a few people."

"Do you think a teacher would go along with something like that?"

"Don't know. But Mrs. Williams is really nice and fun. She might."

"Wow. I never have to pretend to get into trouble. It just happens," I said.

"Don't worry. At least everyone doesn't think you're perfect."

"No danger of that," I said, laughing.

I felt good about the talk I'd had with Sarah. It seemed like I suddenly knew her better. But in a way, I felt bad—I must have been so busy worrying about my life and my involvements that I hadn't even noticed that Sarah wasn't all that happy with hers.

Reputations are funny. You certainly can't judge people solely on them. There's a lot more to a person than the part that shows on the outside—more to Sarah, more to Michael, and more to me. I wondered what my reputation was, anyway. Impetuous? "Hey, Mom," I called downstairs before going to bed, "what does impetuous mean?"

"Oh . . . it means rushing in headlong, being hasty, impulsive, spontaneous. Why?"

"No reason."

I fell asleep thinking about being a rushy, hasty, headlong, impulsive, spontaneous person.

Seventeen

I arrived for Saturday rehearsal raring to go.

Michael arrived with poison ivy. It was all over his hands and arms. His fingers were puffy and oozy.

"What happened to you?" George asked.

"I was getting one of my kittens out of some bushes. Didn't see the poison ivy."

"Well, you'll be all right in time for the performance, but I don't see how you can play today. I'd like you to stay, though."

"Okay."

"Maybe I can talk my friend Thelma into coming over to fill in. She lives close by. I'll see if she's home," George said, heading for the phone.

Michael shrugged, not looking happy about having someone take his place.

"Hey, Michael," George called over his shoulder as

he dialed. "Do you have any Calamine lotion or gauze to treat that mess?"

"No."

"All right, I'll see what I can do."

We got started on the choreography of the "Ugg-A-Wugg" number. Just about everyone but the pirates was in it, and it was good to begin with because it was peppy and got everyone going. Sarah helped the choreographer with the younger kids.

By the time George returned, we were breathless. "Okay, let's break for a minute. I want to see the whole number once you get your wind back." He walked to where Michael was slouched in a seat. "We're in luck, Mike. Thelma can be here in about a half-hour." George sat down in the front row. "All right, while we're resting the Ugg-A-Wugg people, let's have the pirates on stage."

I started to sit down. "Wait a minute, Christy. Do me a favor," George said, reaching into his pocket and pulling out a five-dollar bill. "Take this and see if you can get some Calamine lotion and a roll of gauze at the drugstore."

"Okay," I answered, happy to have the chance to get some fresh air and catch my breath. It was a cloudy, cool day and the autumn air felt good. I wondered what Jeff was doing. Probably at his Saturday college class.

I went up and down the aisles a few times before finding what George wanted. The snacks looked tempting but I stuck to my instructions and just got what George asked for.

I made it back just in time. "All right, pirates, that was

good. Now, all you rested-up Ugg-A-Wuggs, step lively," George ordered. I handed him the change, Michael the bag, and hopped up on the stage. Michael began pouring on the lotion. We should have thought of cotton balls. He was having trouble keeping the Calamine from running onto his clothes and the floor.

Partway through the piano-less number, I looked up and saw a gray-haired woman standing in the doorway. Smiling, she gave a wave to George, who gestured for her to come in. I could see that she didn't want to interrupt us, because she hesitated, then walked slowly, the long way, all around the edges of the theater. When she reached the piano, she bent over and looked at the music. Then she took glasses out of her purse and looked closer. "Hold it a minute," George said to us. "Everybody, this is Thelma. She's going to fill in for Michael today." He turned to Michael and motioned for him to pull up a chair next to the piano. I couldn't hear what George was saying, his back was to us, but Thelma was smiling and Michael was nodding.

Soon Thelma was doing the nodding and Michael was pointing to different places in the music.

"All right, everyone, let's start again. Ready?" George said, looking at Thelma. She pushed her glasses higher on her nose and motioned yes. We began. Thelma made a few mistakes and didn't always have the tempo we were used to, but for someone just filling in, she was very good. Michael would whisper to her at times and she'd nod and smile. In one spot the music had to be played very fast. When we all stopped, Thelma was laughing. "Oh, my goodness, fly you old fingers!" she said. Michael smiled at her.

While we were changing the set for a scene on the pirate ship, Michael took the gauze roll out of the wrapper and started winding it awkwardly around the oozy places on his hands. Seeing that he needed help, Thelma wound it around and between his fingers. To tie it she ripped the end down the center and knotted the two thin strips together. Something she said made Michael laugh. George caught my eye and smiled.

At noon George called a forty-five-minute lunch break. Thelma went home for lunch; the rest of us picnicked in different areas of the theater.

"Hey, Sarah, I forgot a drink. Can I borrow some money to go to 7-Eleven?" I asked.

"I guess. Promise to pay me back though. And would you get me a package of Twinkies?" Sarah held out the money. She was settled comfortably on the floor with friends and seemed happy to have me do her legwork.

"Mom will have a fit—"

"I know," she interrupted, "but a kid should have a Twinkie every so often. It's abnormal and un-American not to."

As I was walking back across the street from the 7-Eleven, I decided it was so nice I'd eat my lunch outside. I went in, tossed Sarah her Twinkie, and headed out into the fresh air. Fall was my favorite season and I didn't want to miss any more of it than necessary. Sitting on the grass and staring off toward the faraway hills as I ate, I was startled to hear someone come up behind me.

"Hi," Jeff said, looking pleased to have surprised me.

I swallowed the bite of sandwich I'd been chewing. "Hi. What are you doing here?" Pound, thump.

"I called your house and your mom told me where you

were." He sat down next to me. Pound, thump—double time. "How's the play going?"

"Good. Except that Michael has poison ivy all over his hands and can't play the piano. We have a substitute."

I offered Jeff some of my soda. "No, thanks." He reached for a twig and flipped it out in front of us. "Today . . . well . . . things weren't too good at my house so I decided to get out for a while." He pulled at the grass and looked off into the distance.

"I'm sorry—I mean about whatever's wrong at home."

"Oh, well . . . it's just something I have to work out with my dad."

"Oh."

"We sort of had a huge argument. My brother and I didn't want to go to a course he'd signed us up for. We told Dad we're not going to suddenly get mushy-brained if we get Saturdays off—we'll learn the stuff eventually. We're sick of being pushed to take all these advanced things. Things were pretty hot there for a while." He was quiet for a moment. I didn't know what to say, so I was quiet too. "Anyway—I always like being with you and I was wondering—when do you finish here?"

When I heard him say he liked being with me, I pounded and thumped like never before. I nearly forgot to answer his question. "About three, I think."

"Good."

"Why good?"

"Well, I thought we could see a movie later. Want to?"

"Sure. When?"

He tossed a clump of grass in the air, smiled, and said,

"Tonight. Let's go to the early show, then we could go out for pizza or something after."

"Okay. I'll have to check with my parents, but it's probably fine." I was trying to sound calm. On the inside I was letting out a gigantic whoop!

"Christy," Sarah called from the doorway, "let's go. We're starting." She looked surprised to see Jeff.

Jeff's bicycle was leaning against the weathered side of the theater, near the door. He opened the door for me, then swung onto his bike and peddled away, no hands. "Talk to you later," he called.

Michael was just scraping the last trace of what looked like apple pie from a paper plate when I walked in. George was doing the same. From the pleased look on Thelma's face, I guessed she'd brought it to them.

"Up and at 'em, everyone. Let's start at the beginning with the nursery scene and see how far we can get," George said.

My mind was darting the rest of the afternoon—from the nursery to Jeff, from the mermaid's lagoon to Jeff, from the pirate ship to Jeff. And when we reached my song, "I Won't Grow Up," I wasn't sure I meant it quite as much as before.

Eighteen

"What movie are you going to see?" Dad asked. I think he was trying to sound relaxed about my going out on a date.

"I don't know yet. We didn't talk about it. But we're going here in town, so it has to be one of those two."

"Just the two of you?" Dad said. Mom looked as though she'd been about to ask the same thing.

"Yes. Isn't that okay?" I said.

"I s'pose so," Dad answered.

"Dad, Mom, don't worry. It's fine," Sarah said. She smiled at me, and I felt like running right upstairs to pay back the money I borrowed, with interest.

Mom had the newspaper. "Well, one's an 'R' and the other's a horror film—another Frankenstein remake. That must be the one. Pleasant dreams." She chuckled, knowing how easily I get scared by those movies.

* * *

"Sarah," I said, standing in the doorway of her room, "what should I wear to the movies?"

"Nothing too fancy. But wear antiperspirant in case you get nervous and sweat."

"Oh, jeez."

"I'm serious. Do it," she said.

Back in my room I pulled out a green rugby shirt and blue jeans, then a white sweater and gray jeans, then a blue Izod and—"Hazel, what do you think? Here, I'll try some things on."

Hazel and I settled on the green rugby and blue jeans. Green's Hazel's favorite color.

"Not good," commented Sarah as she passed my room.

"Why not?"

"'Cause if you do sweat, it'll show easier on a dark top than a light one," she said.

"Oh. So I can't ever wear a dark top on a date?"

"Maybe in colder weather, or maybe if you're positive you won't sweat. But it's risky."

Out came the tops and bottoms again. Hazel and I decided that a white sweater and gray jeans were safe.

The phone rang. "Chris, it's for you," called Mom.

"Hi. Everything okay for the movies?" Jeff asked.

"Fine. Are we seeing the horror one?"

"If that's all right. There isn't much choice."

"It'll be fun."

"Okay. I'll come over at about quarter to six."

While I was showering, Sarah came into the bathroom. "Hey, don't open the door! I have all the hot air tucked in," I complained.

"I just came to offer to help you do your hair," she said.

"Really? Thanks." Sarah's hair always looked good. Maybe she could work a miracle on mine.

Leaving my retainer on my bureau, I came downstairs an hour later looking very unlike Peter Pan. My hair was feathered back and I had eye makeup on. I felt weird. If I'd had time, I'd have probably switched back to the old me. "May I take your picture?" Mom asked.

"No."

"Oh, come on."

"No, No, NO!"

"Okay, okay, but someday you may regret not having a picture of your first date," she said.

Jeff looked perfect. It wasn't that he was especially dressed up or anything; he just looked good. His light-blue shirt with the sleeves partly rolled up went well with his tan and his dark eyes and hair. He wore the same great-fitting jeans he'd had on at the library. And he spoke politely to my parents, which I know they liked. Even Sarah looked impressed. But I don't think anyone noticed his veins but me.

After we got settled in the theater, I realized I had a problem—where to put my hands, or at least the one nearest Jeff. I didn't want to wave it around in an obvious way so he'd think I was hinting that he should hold it. When he got us candy, that settled things for a while, since he held the box between us with one hand, and used the other to eat with. But when we ran out of candy, the problem was back.

I decided to just leave my hand lying out, in a casual

way, on the armrest between us. Nothing happened. Without thinking, I began tapping my fingers. Jeff turned and smiled, then he put his hand over mine. An electric zap went through me, and my face turned hot . . . in the dark it wouldn't show, I hoped. Not knowing whether he was holding my hand because he felt romantic, or because he couldn't stand the tapping, bothered me. But his hand felt great over mine . . . for a while at least. Then my hand started to feel hot. Sarah warned me about sweating, but I didn't think she meant hands.

Jeff got up to get us sodas after a while. As soon as he left, I wiped my hand on my pants and blew on it. The cold cup also cooled it off. I put the hand back on the armrest and he held it again. I guess he didn't care what temperature it was.

Since I couldn't concentrate on the movie, its scariness didn't bother me. Sitting with Jeff and wondering what we'd do after the movie took my attention.

When it ended, Jeff said, "Let's get something to eat. We could get pizza, or hamburgers, or ice cream. What do you feel like?"

"Anything's fine." I wasn't sure I was hungry. Later I'd probably be starving.

"Okay, then let's walk to the pizza place down the road. It's closest."

We ordered two 7-Ups and a medium pizza with extra cheese, then found a table in the corner of the room. We sat down and I discovered a new problem—eating. The pizza smelled great and I was starting to feel hungry. Jeff separated two pieces and put one on each plate. The extra cheese was thick and very stringy. I was afraid of it. I knew that if I took a good-sized bite, I'd end up with strings dangling from my mouth—not a pretty sight. Picking at the crust seemed like the safest idea. Jeff took bite after delicious bite, with no strings attached, but I knew I'd have no such luck.

"You want another drink?" he said, finishing his first one. "I think I'll get one."

"No, thanks. I'm fine."

He got up and walked to the counter, where he stood with his back to me. I looked down at the pizza, then back up at Jeff. The moment seemed right. Quickly I took three large bites.

Then Jeff turned and walked back toward the table, carrying his drink.

Oh, my gosh, I thought. I look just like a chipmunk. I reached for my soda and tried to wash some of the mouthful down.

"The movie was pretty good, didn't you think?" Jeff asked.

"Mmmm," I mumbled, nodding enthusiastically.

"Did you ever see the old black and white original?"

"Nnnn-nnn," I answered, shaking my head and trying to swallow.

A large, black beetle lumbered along the floor by our table. He must have known the weather would be changing soon. "We should catch him," Jeff said. "The bug collection's coming up. He's not going to last long inside here anyway."

I swallowed again. "I know. I'm trying to finish with the mold before I get involved with bugs, though." With a large gulp of soda, I was finally able to speak normally. "But that reminds me. I spoke to Michael about doing a project."

"Good. What kind of project?"

"Oh, I suggested maybe cat responses, or catgut vibration, or something. You know, I really think we were right when we wondered if he's been staying in that house alone, and not with relatives. I think he was there a few nights ago when I was walking our dog." I added the part about the cookies in his lunch.

"You want to check again?"

We got up, leaving two pieces of pizza behind, and this time Jeff held my hand as we walked. We crossed the ball field and headed down Locust Street. Lights were on again at the Taylor house. As we got closer, we could hear music. I recognized one of Justus Taylor's recordings.

"He can't keep this up, Jeff. I'm sure he's alone. It's wrong."

"Should we talk to him?" Jeff asked.

I hesitated. "Yes." We walked up the steps. I let go of Jeff's hand and reached for the doorbell. Then, remembering that it was broken, I knocked. Someone moved inside. I knocked again, and the door opened.

Nineteen

Michael stared at us, seeming to go pale on the spot. "What are you doing here?" His voice sounded tight.

"We were taking a walk and saw you were home," Jeff said, trying to sound natural and friendly.

Michael stood there . . . and we stood there . . . and finally he said, "Want to come in?" I'm sure he hoped we'd say no.

"Sure," we both said at once. He pushed open the door. His hands still had the gauze wrap on them.

The house smelled like canned ravioli and cat food. Dust balls moved along the baseboards as we walked. A bag of potato chips lay open on the footstool. He held up the bag, offering us some. Either it was an especially crackly bag or his hand was shaking.

"No, thanks. We just ate," I said.

There was an awkward silence, and we all just stood there. Then Jeff said, "Nice music."

Michael didn't reply for a minute, then he looked toward the record player and said, "Yeah—thanks. That's a record of my grandfather and a group he used to play with."

"You live with him?" Jeff asked.

"Umm, yes. Well, I did, anyway."

"Not anymore?" I asked. The color in Michael's face seemed to come back—but it still didn't look right. It had turned that ruddy color that usually means a person's awfully uncomfortable.

"No. He broke his hip so he's away for a while." I waited to see if he'd go on. Finally he added, "I'm taking care of the house until he gets back."

"Is that a picture of him?" I said, pointing to a photograph on top of the TV. "And of you when you were younger?" I felt as though I was running for the pryer of the year. If only Mr. Abbot could see me "probing further."

"Yeah."

The record ended and it was quiet again. I was sure Michael was trying to figure out how to get rid of us.

I looked at another picture. "This looks like you, too."

"Me with Justus and my mom," Michael said.

"Your mother lives here too?" asked Jeff. He was turning into a mighty fine prober himself. This felt like the game Twenty Questions. But Michael did seem to be slowly opening up.

Michael walked over to the TV and picked up a postcard propped against a framed picture. "Mom's in Texas right now. She travels a lot." He pointed to more postcards. "She's a singer. Before Justus' group broke up, she sang with them." He paused, looking at the cards. "Now she goes all over. But she comes home sometimes." He looked toward us and added softly, "We just never know when."

Oh, God, I thought. He must be so lonely. How could a kid stand that—not even knowing when his mother would come home?

Jeff studied the postcard from Texas, then looked at Michael. "What about your dad?"

"Never knew him."

"Oh, I'm sorry."

"Michael, uh . . . I have to tell you . . . actually we came because we were worried," I said, trying not to sound as nervous as I really felt about interfering in his life.

"Worried about what?" Michael asked. He rubbed his ear. "Stupid mosquitoes get in here." He was obviously attempting to change the subject. "I wonder if my Calamine lotion works on mosquito bites."

"You're alone here, aren't you?"

"No . . . um, I'm staying with an aunt and uncle. . . ." He scratched his ear again. "I'm just here checking on the house." He sat down and reached for a chip. Then he changed his mind and let it drop back into the bag.

Jeff looked at me. I could tell he didn't believe Michael. Finally he said, "Aw, come on, Michael—the truth."

"Michael, I can't believe you're actually living alone. It's crazy. We're only seventh graders." I decided to just go for it and say it outright. "Jeff and I aren't trying to ruin things for you. But we're worried. Tell us what's going on."

One of Michael's cats sauntered into the room and hopped up on his lap. Michael stroked him quietly. Then he pushed his shaggy hair off his forehead and sighed. Jeff moved the chips off the stool and sat down facing Michael. I sat next to him on the couch.

"What would be wrong with staying with someone?" Jeff said.

"Nothing. Except I don't really have anyone to stay with around here. I mean, no relatives. I just told George that I did so he wouldn't think I was by myself. Before Justus left, we sent my mom a letter to her last address telling her what was going on. Maybe she didn't get it yet or maybe she just can't come right now. Anyway, I'm not telling Justus that—he thinks she's come. He has enough problems without worrying about me."

Michael stroked the cat on his lap. "Besides, we have cats to take care of—five of them. I can't just go off and leave them behind."

I caught a glimpse of one hopping onto the windowsill and settling down behind the curtain.

Michael went on. "This isn't a big deal, being here. And, as I said, it won't be for much longer. Mom should be here any day. And Justus is tough. He'll mend fast and be home soon. He hates to be away and he hates having all the people around him at the convalescent center. He's a really private person." Michael paused and cracked a knuckle. It sounded muffled under the gauze. "Justus wanted to recuperate here. The doctors wouldn't let him, though."

I could see mail in a pile on the table by the door. A lot of it looked like unopened bills. "Where do you get money?" I asked.

"My grandfather set up a joint checking account for him and me a while back. He showed me how to write checks. His Social Security checks automatically go into our account." Michael sounded proud.

"Oh, my gosh, you write checks? I didn't know kids were even allowed to. I wouldn't know how," I said. "What happens if you're caught living alone? I mean, it isn't legal, is it?"

"No, I don't think it is," Jeff answered before Michael had a chance to.

"What about your neighbors? Don't they know?" I said.

Michael shrugged. "People don't pay much attention to each other on this street. Besides, Justus hadn't gotten out much for a while before he fell. They were used to not seeing him."

"Well, the school will probably find out," Jeff said. "You do get in trouble and you're absent a lot. They'll wonder after a while why no one can be reached. Why *are* you absent so much anyway?"

"I have a lot of work to do here. I had a leaky pipe one day and had to plug it up. And another day the heater smelled weird. I wasn't sure if I should call someone or not. And I had to stay home another time to wait for the piano tuner. We always have him come in the fall."

"Even now, with all *this* going on, you had the piano tuned?" I said.

"It's important to Justus. So I made sure it was done."

"But in school, why don't you do your assignments?" I asked. Probe, probe.

Michael sighed. "Oh, I don't know. I don't have much time for schoolwork—and once I leave school, I pretty much put it out of my head. I work on my music, go see Justus, or do jobs around here. I'm not real organized. And I have trouble concentrating on homework. When someone else was around, I did a little better."

"You do so well at play practice. You're fantastic," I said.

"Yeah, well, music isn't work for me—it's the kind of thing I like doing. Anything with music comes easy for me." He smiled.

We were all quiet for a moment. The only sound was a thump from another room—a cat must have jumped down from somewhere. "Okay, now that you both know—now what?" He looked from me to Jeff, then cracked another knuckle.

"You're managing," Jeff said, "and you could probably keep it up for a while longer. But you shouldn't. You shouldn't have to."

"Something could happen. I mean, if it were me, I know I wouldn't know what to do if something really big went wrong. I couldn't do what you're doing," I said, touching his arm with my hand.

Michael sighed again and leaned back against the cushions of the sofa. We were all quiet. Then he said, "Well, nothing major has gone wrong yet. And I told you I'm not telling Justus that Mom's not here. He thinks she just isn't feeling well right now and will visit him when she's better. Once the mail catches up with her, she'll be here." The cat jumped off his lap and ran out through the door.

"I think you should start thinking of another way to handle this whole thing. It's already gone on much longer than you planned," Jeff said.

"We have to go, Michael. I told my folks I'd be home about now. But try to think. Isn't there a relative somewhere who could come here and stay with you?"

"Not that I know of." Michael picked up a soda can near the sofa and squeezed it. "You didn't answer the question—now that you two know, what are you going to do?"

"Well," I said, looking at Jeff, "maybe we should all work on the solution. I'm sure there is one. Do you think George could help?"

"Don't know."

"Do you trust him?"

"Maybe."

"Well, think about that. We'll talk again on Monday," I said.

"Mike, we'll see you," Jeff said, opening the front door.

Walking home I said, "I never knew someone my age with a checking account, did you?"

"Nope."

"You know, Michael is in such a bad spot. He wants to handle things alone—but he can't. It's too much."

"Yeah. It is," Jeff said.

"Michael is really complicated, and . . . I don't know, but it seems that maybe not doing his work, then walking out of class . . . well, he's sort of drawing attention to himself. It seems . . . it's like he had to show that he was having problems." I paused, trying to straighten things out in my mind. "Michael is pretty grown up, but he's still a kid too. And he must feel so alone."

"I think he's scared, too. I'm sure the school will figure things out before much longer. He'd be better off having a friend help him than waiting until the school does something. I suppose it's possible he could be sent to a foster home or institution."

I shivered. "Oh, no. Poor Michael. And poor Justus, too. They'd both be so worried about each other."

We walked without talking for a few minutes. Then, feeling guilty, I said, "I wonder if he's angry with us for poking into his business."

"My guess is that he's relieved."

"Do you really think his mom will come home? It's sad that he waits and waits," I said.

"I looked at that postcard from Texas. The postmark was seven and a half months old."

"That's awful. Poor Michael." I stopped walking. "Jeff, do you think we're taking a chance, not telling someone right away?"

Jeff reached for my hand. "For now, he's managing. I think he's okay—not happy, but okay. I think he's seeing now that he needs an adult to help supervise and organize things. You're nice to worry about him, Chris." Jeff lifted my hand and kissed it.

Jeff was nice to worry about him, too . . . and I was sure I'd remember that kiss for a very long time.

Twenty

"My, you're an early one, Miss Swan," Mr. Abbot said, looking up from a stack of quiz papers. "Is there a problem?"

"Well, yes. It's not mine really, but . . ."

Mr. Abbot smiled. For the first time I noticed the smile lines around his eyes. "Whose problem shall we try to deal with?"

I took a deep breath. "Michael Taylor's."

"Aahh." He looked back down at his papers. I shouldn't have come, I knew it. Most likely Mr. Abbot was still furious about what Michael did.

"This probably isn't a good time for you," I said, stepping backward and turning to go.

"Any student who makes an effort to confer with me first thing Monday morning deserves my attention. Now, tell me what's on your mind."

What was on my mind right then was that I shouldn't

be there. Too late. "Well . . . you know that Michael has a lot of problems," I began hesitantly.

"I do," Mr. Abbot said.

"And you're probably still angry with him for what he did."

"Angry . . . no."

"You're not? Oh." I hadn't expected that response from him. "Well," I stumbled on, "he's going to try in science now. He told me he was going to do a project."

"Good," he replied. "That's very good."

"And I know I'm not minding my own business . . ."

"You aren't," he said. But he didn't sound annoyed. I noticed his smile wrinkles again.

"I sometimes don't, but . . ."

"But?"

"But I came to ask you if maybe you could not be too hard on him," I finally blurted out. Taking a deep breath, I went on, talking fast. "You know, he's a surprising person. Did you realize that he's a fantastic musician? And his grandfather, Justus Taylor, was once a pretty famous jazz pianist."

"Well, what do you know." Mr. Abbot sighed, leaning back in his chair. "I never made the connection. What a coincidence. My wife and I were fans of Justus Taylor's."

"You were? Well, Michael was taught by Justus and you should hear him play. He's amazing."

"Does he play here in school?"

"I don't know about school, but he plays for the theater group I'm in. He accompanies us."

"Which group is that? Not George Harrington's, at the old Forum Theater, by any chance," he said.

"Yes . . . why? Do you know George?"

"For years. In fact, my wife, Thelma, helped him out last Saturday. She was very impressed with the production, by the way."

"My gosh. Is Thelma your wife? That's so amazing. It was Michael she filled in for. Did she tell you?"

"It never occurred to me to ask. She just said how much she enjoyed her day."

I explained about Justus and his broken hip, and about Michael's mother being away. But I didn't say that there was no other adult around. "I don't think he was being mean when he walked out on you," I said, as Mr. Abbot seemed to be pulling his chin in thought. "I don't know why he did it. I guess maybe he was just frustrated. And maybe he needed someone to see that. I'm not sure, but that could be why he's acting the way he is."

The bell rang. "Thank you, Christy. I'll keep in mind what you've told me."

"Oh . . . good. Thank you."

"By the way, how's the mold coming along?"

"Pretty good, thanks." I turned to leave the room, then paused by the door. Mr. Abbot smiled and gave a half-wave. "'Bye," I said.

Things were bound to be better in science today.

The rest of the morning I looked forward to seeing Jeff and had trouble thinking of much else. Lizzie wanted to know all about Saturday night. Some things I kept to myself.

"What'd you do after the movie?" Lizzie asked as she stuffed her jeans into her gym locker.

"We had something to eat and took a walk."

"And?"

"And . . . oh, my gosh," I gasped. "I forgot my gym clothes!"

"Are you sure? Keep looking."

"I'm sure. I had them this morning, but when I went downstairs to let Beezer inside, I left them on top of the dryer. Ohhh no." I slumped to the bench and stared at my empty gym locker. "I wish I had time to find Sarah and get her combination so I could borrow her stuff. There isn't time, right?"

"You wouldn't make it. You'll have to borrow some things from Ms. Bolen."

"Great. She'll just love that. Wish me luck." I backed toward the door. "If I don't come back in three minutes, send a rescue squad." I slinked down the short corridor leading to Ms. Bolen's office.

Her back was to me as I stood in the doorway. She was reaching for some jump ropes hanging on a hook beside her desk.

"Ms. Bolen?" I said in my most polite voice.

"Uh-huh," she answered, not turning around.

"I had to rush this morning to come in early and speak to a teacher, and somehow, with all the hurrying, I left my gym clothes home. I'm sorry."

She began to turn and I cringed. "Ah, Swan. Gym doesn't appear to be your thing, does it?"

I didn't think it would help matters to say, "Well, actually, Ms. Bolen, I'd always liked gym, and done well in it, before having you as a teacher." I kept quiet.

"You'll have to borrow some things. Look in that box over there," she said, pointing. "And you have a check mark."

Four minutes later I clomped into the gym wearing large orange sneakers and baggy gym shorts. LOANERS was painted across the tops of the sneakers and across the rear of the shorts. Once again I was grateful that Jeff was in a different gym class.

Mr. Norden winked. "Those loaners are beauties, aren't they? Don't worry, you're not the first or last student to wear them." He blew his whistle for his squad to gather.

I wondered if when Michael forgets his gym clothes, they give him ones marked "loner."

After lunch I stopped at my locker to drop off some things and get my science and math books. The halls were crowded and I had to be careful not to get jostled. If I did, I might bump something into the small mold colony still growing in the corner. I was protecting it, but with everything else going on, I kept forgetting to do something with it. It needed to be indentified. I was afraid I'd kill it if I moved it out of there, so there it sat, day after day, carefully guarded. I couldn't help feeling almost fond of it; after all, it was part of the original mold that got me started on the project. There's nothing like the first—it's special.

"You really got a mold experiment in there?" said a voice behind me. Mr. Johnson stood looking at my sign: "*DANGER*—mold experiment in progress." I smiled at Mr. Johnson, remembering how helpful he'd been to me that first week of school.

"The principal asked me about it," he said. "She thought maybe it was a joke. But if it isn't, I'm supposed to disinfect the locker."

"Oh, no! Could you please just give me until tomorrow, Mr. Johnson? I haven't had time to do anything with it, but it's part of my science project and I promise to get it out tomorrow. All right? Please?"

"Yeah. Okay. Let me know when you're done." He smiled and gave my shoulder a friendly pat.

"Thank you very much. Have a nice afternoon, Mr. Johnson."

I made my way through the swarming hall to science. Jeff looked up and grinned as I walked in. Pound, thump.

Michael sat at his desk. The guidance counselor must have made some impression on him because he had his science book open and was reading. His clothes looked rumpled, but not as dirty as they'd seemed before. Maybe he'd finally done some laundry over the weekend. He still had Calamine lotion all over his hands.

Mr. Abbot was opening cabinets and bringing out what teachers call "visual aids." There were a couple of study prints of marine life, four microscopes, and some chunks of what looked like coral.

Beth Roman was taking advantage of every last minute to talk before Mr. Abbot began class. "*Loved* your outfit in gym today, Christy," she said, rolling her eyes.

"I'm a trend-setter." I grinned. No way would I let her get to me.

"All right, class," said Mr. Abbot. Beth began to say one last thing, but Mr. Abbot cut her off. "Miss Roman, we are beginning now. If you cannot resist the urge to talk, you will have to move to the back of the room." Beth looked behind her to where he was pointing. "That's right," said Mr. Abbot, "next to the skeleton." Beth let out a squeal. Mr. Abbot chuckled. "Now, let's begin. We will be talking about marine life today, specifically small invertebrates."

Michael looked up. I smiled at him. I think he smiled back. It was hard to tell, he did it so fast.

"We will start by reviewing what was included in last night's chapter," Mr. Abbot said, flipping to that section of the book.

Todd was called on to describe the anemone. Eric Sutton's knowledge of coral polyps was not impressive and so Lizzie was asked to add what she knew. I did what I could with algae.

"Who can explain what an atoll is?" Mr. Abbot asked. He looked for a volunteer. There was none. Glancing at Michael he must have noticed that Michael's book was opened to the right page. "Michael, can you tell us?"

Michael shifted uncomfortably in his seat and looked down at the book. "Ummm . . . an atoll is . . ." He looked up, as if he weren't sure if it was all right to read the definition. Mr. Abbot nodded. Michael went on. "An atoll is a ring-shaped reef formed by tiny dead marines."

Peals of laughter.

Giggles.

Shrieks.

Holding of bellies.

"Did they get there on tiny battleships?" Andy called out.

"They died fighting teeny tiny wars!" added Beth hysterically.

Michael clenched his jaw and looked as if he wished he were dead. Jeff and Lizzie looked quietly sympathetic.

"Hold it. Enough!" Mr. Abbot said firmly. The room became quiet. "That was an easy error to make. The way the sentence was placed on the page, one could easily skip the last word, 'animals,' on the first reading. 'Atolls are formed by tiny marine *animals*,' or whatever the exact wording was. A simple mistake, Michael."

Mr. Abbot strode to the blackboard and while he drew a picture of an atoll, with a lagoon in the middle, kids looked at each other and shrugged in disbelief. Mr. Abbot defending Michael was not what they expected.

I don't think it was what Michael expected either. But the result was good. He paid attention for the rest of the period and was the first to look through a microscope.

Jeff touched my hand as he stood behind me in line to look at algae. I felt electrified.

When the bell rang, Mr. Abbot said, "All right. That's it for today. A reminder—your projects are due in two weeks. Tomorrow be prepared to meet with me individually to discuss your progress."

As kids collected their things, Michael hung back.

"Come on, Christy," whispered Lizzie, "I want to walk behind Todd. But we'll lose him if we don't hurry."

I looked over my shoulder as we left the room. Michael was standing by Mr. Abbot's desk. "I have an idea for a project," I heard him say.

Twenty-one

The next few days went well. Jeff called every night, Mr. Abbot and Michael seemed to be at peace, and the play was really shaping up. I even managed to get my mold out of the locker before it was exterminated. It turned out to be pretty average mold, and not the Nobel Prize sort I'd hoped for.

Columbus Day was a school holiday, so we got an extra full day of rehearsing. With the play only a little more than a week away, we practiced in costumes so we could get used to the way they felt.

At the noon break a bunch of us walked across the street to get drinks and snacks. It was funny being in costume in the outside world, and we were pretty noisy and keyed up. Stanley and Charles stayed in character as Captain Hook and Smee and drew lots of stares and chuckles.

"I'll sink me hook into ya, Smee, unless ya fetch me that sack of pretzels," ordered Stanley.

"Aye-aye, Captain," replied Charles, jumping to obey and knocking several bags of chips from the shelf.

"Faster, matey!" Stanley swiped at Charles with his hook.

We paid for the food, then headed back across the street to the theater. Stanley gave me a poke. "Step lively, Pan."

"Prepare to meet thy doom, Hook!" I yelled, giving him a kick in the seat.

"Go get him, Peter! Don't let that nasty hook scare ya," cheered Charles. We were pretty noisy by the time we reached the theater.

When we walked in the door, laughing, I noticed a bright cookie tin on top of the piano. Even before I saw her, I knew Thelma was back. "Help yourselves, kids," she said, pointing to the tin. Michael was already chewing on one cookie and had several more stacked at one end of the keyboard.

We quieted down. I think it was out of respect for Thelma. Her eyes were bright as she talked excitedly to Michael. I heard the name Justus mentioned and knew she was telling Michael what a fan she was. He grinned at her. I'd never seen a grin like that on his face before.

During the rest of the rehearsal, Michael and Thelma sat side by side on the piano bench. Michael played most of the time, but once in a while Thelma would take a turn, probably to give his sore-looking hands a rest. The poison ivy was better but not completely gone.

It was nearly time to quit when George said, "Okay, kids, the last thing we'll do today is run through the beginning of the first act one last time. We want to dazzle the audience with our opener. Places everyone."

We reached the part where Peter comes into the Darlings' nursery to look for his shadow and meets Wendy. She sews on the shadow and then Peter bursts into "I Gotta Crow." During that number I'm supposed to strut about looking cocky and conceited, and several times I'm supposed to hop onto chairs and stools. At the end, for my big crowing finale, I hop onto Wendy's bed. Everything was going fine until the final part. I leaped onto Wendy's bed and did a spectacular bit of crowing, and then, when the rest of the cast and crew was applauding, I hopped backward to the floor. Wendy's sewing basket was still there from when she had sewn on the shadow, and I landed smack on top of it.

I wobbled, then the next thing I knew, I was on the floor with my left arm underneath me. "Owwww!" A sharp pain was shooting through my wrist. At first people laughed because it was such a comical finish. But when I didn't pop up, they all went quiet.

George was the first to move. "Christy, take it easy," he said, scrambling up onto the stage.

Sarah dashed out from the wings. "You really hurt yourself, didn't you?" Sisters can usually tell when you're faking and when you're not. She knelt beside me and put her arm on my shoulder.

"Most of me is all right," I answered, "but my wrist hurts."

"Let's look at it," George said. He felt my arm and wrist carefully. "I can't really tell anything, Chris. Can you bend it?"

I tried. It ached with zaps of sharp pain. "It's not right."

"Everyone, listen. We'll stop for today. I want you to

clean up. Christy, you just sit still. Sarah, is someone coming to pick you two up?"

"Yes," she said, glancing at the clock on the wall. "Probably someone's left already, but I'll call to be sure." She paused, looking at me. "She looks really white, George."

I was beginning to feel waves of nausea.

"Yeah, a bit. But she'll be fine. I'm going to supervise the cleanup, Chris. Sit tight," George said.

Thelma climbed the steps by the side of the stage and walked over to me. She sat on Wendy's bed. "My, that was some dramatic finish! George said to dazzle, but I don't think you needed to go that far." Thelma smiled at me and patted my back gently. "How do you feel, dear?"

"My wrist aches. Mostly that's all."

"Well, I'll just sit here with you until one of your parents gets here." Thelma patted me again. I kind of felt like leaning against her; she seemed soft and warm.

Michael hopped up on the stage. "I could get you some ice or something."

"No, thanks."

"Nothing?"

"No, thanks."

Michael smiled. "Okay then—one thing I could probably do for you is get you some mold. I bet I've got some around."

"I'll bet you do, too," I answered, laughing.

Thelma looked confused. "He's talking about my science project," I explained.

"Oh," she said. "I have connections in that area. Now don't you worry about that project for the time being." She patted me again.

It was Michael's turn to look confused. "Michael, you're not going to believe this. Thelma's last name is Abbot. She's married to Mr. Abbot," I explained.

Michael was speechless for a moment. His face looked a little red.

"Christy, Mom's here," called Sarah. "Do you need help?"

"No, I'm coming." But Thelma and Michael ended up steadying me. At first I didn't think they needed to, then I realized how weird I felt. "Thanks," I said. "See you soon."

Mom hurried over to me. She didn't panic, but she frowned as she felt my wrist. "I can't tell anything, but let's go to the hospital," she said. George volunteered to drop Sarah off and let Dad know what we were doing.

As we rode to the emergency room, I said, "It can't be broken. No way. Things like this don't happen to me." A minute later I added, "Oh, my gosh, I'd be a bystander! I couldn't stand that. It's not broken." I insisted, feeling the panic building.

"I hope not, too," Mom said, smiling at me.

The X rays were taken. The verdict was a shock. The wrist was fractured. I was sure there was a mistake. Those bones in the X rays must have been someone else's. But the doctor acted as if they were definitely mine.

"Here's the spot. Not good." He pointed out the fracture on one of the X rays . . . one with *my* name on it. Then he went on to compare my wrist to a green twig which had been damaged by a hard twist. I tried not to hear him.

"This is just great," I muttered. "How can I be Peter Pan? How can I do my hair? Take a shower? Ride my bike?" I felt like stomping. "My life has been ruined by a stupid sewing basket."

"Christy, your life has certainly not been ruined. I understand your frustration, but I hardly expect you to—"

"*Mom*, do you honestly think an audience will believe in a one-armed Peter Pan? I'll be out of the play."

The doctor cleared his throat. I guess he figured we were ignoring him. I'd have liked to. "Mrs. Swan, I am going to put a removable cast, a sturdy splint really, on your daughter's arm for tonight. I think it would be best to wait until tomorrow to have her regular doctor, or an orthopedist, put the cast on . . . It's not my specialty."

"Neither is good news," I mumbled to myself.

"I'm going to write a prescription for a painkiller," he said. "She'll probably have some discomfort tonight."

Flowers were on the table by the door when I walked in the house. I looked at Dad and smiled. "Thanks, Dad. That was nice."

"I'd like to take credit for them, but I cannot tell a lie. Your friend Jeff brought them over."

"Really?" I leaned over and smelled the flowers. They were the first I'd ever been given. "How'd he find out about my wrist?" Maybe it was psychic love.

"Sarah told him when he called. Then he rode his bike over and left these. How does the wrist feel? Are you in any pain?"

"What? Uh, no . . . well, some. It's okay though." I bent down and smelled the flowers again. "I want to keep these in my room." I carried the vase, one-handed, upstairs. "Company, Hazel. Aren't they pretty?" I hoped Hazel wasn't jealous.

I was too tired for supper. Mom, Dad, and Sarah, followed by Beezer, trooped up to my room and sat with me for a few minutes before they ate dinner. "You had quite a day, Christy," said Dad. "I hope you can get some sleep."

Mom brought me a painkiller and some juice. "Call me if you need anything during the night," she said as she smoothed the covers and slid an extra pillow under my arm. She and Dad each gave me a kiss and went downstairs.

"Hey, shrimp," Sarah said. "You know, I've never gotten flowers from a boy. You're ahead of me there. Jeff's a nice guy. You're lucky."

"Thanks. I wonder if he'll call again tonight. If he does, please tell him I said thank you for the flowers."

"Okay. Good night." She paused in the doorway. "You know, Chris, I've been wanting to tell you this for a long while—I'm impressed by you."

"What?"

Sarah looked embarrassed, but she went on. "You're a neat person. You have a lot going for you. I'm even glad you're my sister."

"Thank you." Boy, was I amazed. Had she suffered from a severe bump on the head while I was gone?

"I know I've been mean and sarcastic sometimes; I guess it's a stage. I never used to be like that, so I hope it's not the real me. It should pass. You might even get into it soon. Let's hope I'm done with it by then, because two in the house at the same time would be a bit much," she said, laughing.

"Yeah, it would," I agreed. "Mom and Dad would probably pack up and move."

"Well, I hope you sleep all right. See you in the morning." She closed my door and I was alone with the aching. The doctor was right—I did need painkillers. The trouble was, I needed better ones than he prescribed. No matter what position I was in, the wrist ached. I hardly got any sleep. But I did get a lot of thinking done. I thought about getting the wrist set in the morning, and whether it would hurt. Then I thought about what Sarah had said and how I was really glad she had. I hoped the magic spell wouldn't be broken by morning. Then I thought about Jeff and the flowers, about the play, about mold, about Michael, and about Thelma and Mr. Abbot. My thoughts weren't orderly, flowing neatly from one separate subject to the next—they were jumbled and swirled, as if my mind were an eggbeater mixing everything together.

I looked at Hazel. She looked sympathetic. "Boy, life gets complicated, Hazel." Being a plant has its advantages. Or even being Beezer for a day would be nice. Actually being Beezer and being a plant aren't too different.

My thoughts returned to Michael. His problems were such big ones. "Michael sure does need friends right now. Hazel, do you have any plant pals who might like to move in over there?"

I wondered if Justus Taylor's nights were like this. His pain probably kept him awake, too. What did he think about? His daughter? His music? Or when he'd be able to get home to Michael. I hoped he knew Michael had some friends now.

Twenty-two

It hurt when the cast was put on. Dr. Hutchinson had to position the wristbones before he could wrap the warm, wet strips around my arm. At least it hurt less than it had the night before when I could have sworn a Mack truck had barreled through my room and run over my arm.

"Don't worry about how this'll look when the cast comes off," said Dr. Hutchinson.

"What do you mean?" I asked.

"Your arm will be dry and pruny," he said matter-of-factly.

"What? That's disgusting."

"Don't look so alarmed," Dad said, winking at Dr. Hutchinson, who was an old friend of his. "It won't really look pruny."

"It'll look more lizardy," he said, straight-faced. Then I guess he couldn't stand the way I sort of sagged when he said that, because he added, "Just kidding, just kidding." He gave my shoulder a gentle squeeze. "It'll be as good as new in no time."

"Yup. We were only kidding," Dr. Hutchinson said.

I wasn't sure if they were or not. I was worried. Jeff, with his perfect arms, might be repulsed by my reptilian one.

Dad and I stopped for a quick hamburger, then headed for school. "By the way, you had some calls last night. George called to see how you were and asked for you to get in touch with him later today," Dad said as we drove along.

I didn't say anything. I just turned my head and stared out the window. I didn't want to hear what George had to tell me.

"Mrs. Abbot called, too, and said she hopes you're feeling better. She also said she's very impressed by your talent."

"She did? She's a really nice person."

"Yes, she sounds that way. And . . . there was one more call." Dad smiled and waited. Then he began humming.

"Come on, cut it out. Who was it?" I asked.

"Who? Well . . . Hmmmm."

"DAD!"

"Okay, okay. It was Jeff. He wanted to know how you were and he said he'd see you today."

I smiled, then looked down at my cast. I probably wasn't going to be playing the part of a boy who wouldn't grow up, but it wasn't so bad being a girl who would.

We pulled into the circle in front of the school. "Are you sure you feel up to being here?" Dad asked.

"I think so. I don't want to have to make up all the work."

"When I was a kid, I always wanted to walk into school with a cast on," Dad said.

I knew what he meant, but now that I'd probably lose my part in the play and have to be a bystander for weeks, it didn't seem like such a neat thing.

Dad walked in with me to sign me in late. We waited by the counter for Mrs. Wolcott, the school secretary, who was standing in the doorway of the principal's office with her back to us. "Do you mean to tell me that his parents have never been contacted? How did that happen? It's been a couple of weeks since he walked out of Bill Abbot's class," Mrs. Hoyt, the principal, said.

My stomach jumped. I was afraid I knew who they were talking about. I looked up at Dad. If he had any idea, he didn't show it.

"I know that," answered Mrs. Wolcott, "but I tried. For several days straight I called and had no luck reaching anyone. And with all the turmoil created by the asbestos inspection, then the fingerprinting project, and finally all the kids trooping through the office to see the nurse for the scoliosis screening, it got pushed aside. I'm sorry. But at least he's been seen by Guidance."

"True, and I gather that's gone fairly well," said Mrs. Hoyt. "But we still need to speak with his parents. I should have followed up myself, but somehow it slipped by me, too. Well, let's be sure to make contacting the Taylors a priority."

I felt my insides starting to shake. Dad nudged me. "Are they talking about Michael, the piano player?"

"Oh, boy . . ." I mumbled.

Michael had to be warned. If he were caught living alone, there was no telling what would happen.

Twenty-three

"'Bye, Dad. Thanks very much. See you after school," I said, backing out of the office.

Dad had signed me in and explained about my wrist and that I'd probably be out of gym for a while. Ms. Bolen would love that.

I stopped at my locker, then headed straight for the cafeteria, carrying the few books I could hold in one arm. Lunch period was almost over, but my friends would still be there and I was anxious to try to find Michael. Hesitating by the door, I looked around for him. But Lizzie spotted me first.

"Oh, my gosh!" cried Lizzie, running over to me. "You really did break something. People said so, but I didn't know if it was true. Another Swan dive?"

"Yeah. Pretty klutzy, huh?" I answered, looking over her shoulder for Michael.

"Now what? Can you still be Peter Pan?" Lizzie asked.

"Doubt it. I'd look pretty dumb."

"Hi, Chris. How are you feeling?" said a voice behind me. Pound, thump. I turned, feeling my face burn, to see Jeff looking concerned. I glanced down at my clunky arm, then at his wonderful ones—I loved the way his looked with the sleeves rolled up.

"I'm fine really. Thanks for the flowers. That was nice," I said softly.

It wasn't so soft that Lizzie couldn't hear, and her eyes widened as she looked from me to Jeff and back again.

Jeff smiled. "You're welcome. I'm glad you're okay."

I thought about being okay for a moment. With one wobble of the sewing basket, my chance at stardom went crash, but I had a lot of other good things in my life, so I guess I should be okay.

"There's the bell. I'll see you in science, Chris," Jeff said, touching my shoulder before heading back to his table. I tingled. Yes, I was definitely okay.

As people began to clear out of the cafeteria, I glanced around, but still didn't see Michael. I had to get to him soon. I wished I'd told Jeff what I'd heard in the office. Maybe he'd be able to warn him.

By the time I got to science class, my cast was covered with signatures . . . I was tired of the instant celebrity bit and was tempted to make up juicy stories to break the monotony of telling about my fall.

Mr. Abbot smiled as I walked into class. "Well, I hear you had a spectacular finish to one of your numbers yesterday. I'm sorry you hurt yourself."

"Oh, well, you know how they always say, 'Break a

leg' in show business. I got confused and broke my wrist. I've gotta learn to follow directions . . . and maybe learn to look before I leap (and crow)."

Mr. Abbot chuckled. A few minutes later class was under way. I wondered when I'd have a chance to let Michael know that the office was going to try to reach his family. I glanced at him. He was diagramming something to do with his project.

I tried to think how I was going to tell him. He already had so much pressure—I hated adding more. I knew that he had to be convinced to tell an adult, but it might be hard to persuade him to do that. And what if I talked him into doing something that would only make matters worse? That might mean disaster for Michael.

"Psssst, Michael," I whispered as class was ending and kids were gathering up books and papers to leave. "I have to talk to you. Wait outside the door."

He looked puzzled.

Jeff came over to me and I asked him to wait with me a minute. Maybe he'd have an idea. Lizzie was in a rush to follow Todd, so she went on ahead.

"You have to do something *fast,*" I said to Michael a minute later. "I overheard Mrs. Hoyt tell Mrs. Wolcott to contact your family. There was a slipup before, but it sounded like they were determined to follow through this time."

"If they've taken this long to do anything, I doubt they'll move very fast," Michael answered.

"Yes, they *will.* I heard them say it would be done *right away*. You've got to do something . . . *now,*" I said, feeling the panic building.

Michael rubbed his neck, then said, "Maybe I should

just go home now and stay there until someone calls. Then I can use a different voice and pretend to be my mother. That should settle things."

"But what if they want a conference with your mother in person?" Jeff said. "They might insist on that. You've been seeing the guidance counselor."

"I could just say that's impossible," Michael answered. "Besides, I just remembered that it'll take them a while to get anywhere because when I filled out that pupil-information card in the beginning of the year, I put down a lot of phony numbers."

"The phony numbers may make them suspicious. And sometimes they send social workers to the house anyway," Jeff said.

"I doubt they ever send people to your house," Michael muttered.

"No, it's true. They do. My mother's a social worker," Jeff replied.

"Oh." Michael jammed his hands into his pockets and closed his eyes for a moment.

"Look," I said, "there must be an adult you could talk to, someone you trust." I was beginning to feel frantic.

Jeff nodded. "There's no telling what'll happen if you're caught alone. You could get sent to some God-awful place."

Michael began to sweat. He kicked at the bottom of the door with the worn toe of his sneaker.

"Michael, *pleeeeeeease,*" I begged. "Look, maybe we should just go to my parents. Okay?"

"No . . . don't know them . . . Uh . . . I guess I'll talk to George." He pushed his hair back from off his forehead.

Jeff glanced at me and looked relieved. We watched Michael turn and walk slowly down the hall. I felt relieved too . . . for a moment. Then a new worry rose insidc me. George would want to help, I knew that, but he might not be able to. What if he made things worse? Would it be my fault for pushing Michael into telling?

I had time at home that afternoon. We had no play practice. Some group had rented the theater for a special program. I knew I had to talk to George about my wrist. It was something I did not want to do. I didn't want to hear what he'd have to say. As I took the phone book out of the drawer in the kitchen and looked up his number, I thought of Michael. I hoped he'd gotten in touch with George. Taking a deep breath, I dialed. It rang, but no one answered. I dialed again, in case I'd gotten the wrong number. Still no answer.

Just as I hung up, the phone rang. It was Lizzie. "Guess what!" she squealed.

"What?"

"Todd walked part of the way home with me, and he asked me to go to his soccer game on Saturday! Isn't that great?"

"Yeah, that is. Congratulations—sounds as if he likes you. That's terrific," I said.

"Ooops—my mother needs to use the phone. I'll have to call you back later. I'm so excited. Can't wait until Saturday! Talk to you soon."

"'Bye."

As I was hanging up the phone again, the doorbell rang. I started toward the door, then stopped. Through the thin white curtains I could make out the shape of a boy. Ordinarily, boys, all shapes and sizes, come to see Sarah, not me, and I don't pay much attention. But this shape was a shape I'd know anywhere. It was Jeff's.

I stood in the middle of the living room, torn between wanting to fling open the door and wanting to dash upstairs and make myself glamorous. The door won. What would be the point of fixing myself up only to find he'd given up waiting and left?

I pushed my hair into place as best I could, tucked in my shirt, using one hand, and went to the door.

"Hi. I was out delivering my papers and came over to see if you're really all right."

"Yup. I am."

He smiled . . . I smiled . . . and we stood there.

"Want to come in?"

"Sure."

"I was just trying to call George about the play. I'm sure I'm out of it now, but he may need me to help get someone else ready to take over my part," I said, trying not to sound as if it mattered.

We sat down on the couch. Jeff reached over and touched my cast. "That was a great part. It's too bad."

I could swear I could feel his touch right through the plaster. Slowly he drew his fingers along the cast until he touched my hand. It was pretty hard to feel sorry for myself under those conditions.

"You know, I am a little upset about losing the part, but I think a couple of weeks ago it would have been worse. Now there are other things more important than whether I play a lead role. I mean, there's Michael. What happens to him matters much more."

"You've done a lot to help him."

"But . . ." I said, pulling at a loose thread on one of the cushions, "but what if I advised Michael the wrong way? Just because I had a lead role in a play doesn't give me the right to take a lead role in Michael's private life. George isn't home. What if he's out right at this very moment signing Michael into a foster home or an institution? It would be my fault."

"Look, Chris, don't act like you've sealed his fate. You're not *that* powerful." He laughed and squeezed my hand. "Sometimes all you can do is try to make things better for someone. You can't always change things or have them the way you want," Jeff said.

"Mmmm. Yeah, I guess that's right. Well, I still keep saying to myself, 'M.Y.O.B.'"

"What?"

"Mind your own business."

Jeff leaned over and kissed me gently. "I'll be your business. How's that?" He kissed even better than he held hands.

"That's fine," I squeaked. My heart was thumping and lightning bolts were zinging through me.

"I'd sign your cast, but I can't really write what I'd like to, not on there anyway, where everyone could see it," he said, getting up. "I have to finish delivering my papers."

"You do?"

"Yeah, sorry. But I'll see you tomorrow." He tapped my cast with his finger. "And *don't* spend all night worrying. You did your best to help Michael. The rest is up to other people."

He left and I sat back down on the couch. I put my

hand on the spot where he'd been. My head swirled—my good feelings about Jeff and my worried feelings about Michael spun round and round. I rubbed my forehead, wishing I could stop the motion in my mind and just focus on the wonderful fact that Jeff liked me.

Twenty-four

The next day Mr. Abbot was absent. Science was dull, but at least I had a chance to talk with Michael. Near the end of the period, when the substitute had run out of things to do, I leaned over toward Michael. "So? Did you reach George?"

"Yeah. I called him when I got home and he came right over. We talked for a long time."

"And?"

"And he said he'd try to figure something out. He'll talk to me again as soon as he has an answer. Maybe today."

"Probably at practice this afternoon." It looked like Michael and I were both going to have talks with George.

Maybe with George's time being taken up with Michael's problem, he hadn't had a chance to find a new

Peter Pan. Not likely, but I've always been a good hoper.

I didn't have much to say on the way to rehearsal. Sarah chattered about a cute new boy who had just moved to town and was in her homeroom. She was planning ways to make him feel welcome. No one could make a guy feel comfortable like Sarah could.

I asked her if she'd ever done her fake getting-into-trouble routine in math class.

"Not yet, but I still might."

Dad looked confused, so she explained and he thought it was pretty funny.

The cast on my wrist caused some commotion when I walked in. I heard a couple of kids wonder out loud what was going to happen to my role.

"All right, everyone, have a seat," said George. He hopped up on the stage and sat with his legs dangling over the side. "Quiet now." He paused for what felt like an awfully long time. "Okay, as you can see, Peter Pan had a crash landing."

Oh-oh, here it comes, I thought. Don't be a wimp, Chris.

"Nowhere in the stage notes does it say that Peter has to wear short sleeves," George went on.

What was he saying? My icy stomach felt confused.

"With long sleeves, the cast could be hidden, for the most part," he continued. "If Sir James M. Barrie were to see Christy Swan in the title role of his play, I know he'd be thrilled by her performance, cast or no cast."

I blushed and stared at my sneakers.

"That said"—George gave another of his dramatic pauses—"if you believe in Christy, clap your hands!"

They clapped.

Michael smiled.

So did Sarah.

I may have grown up enough not to have *needed* the role, but I sure was happy to have it.

"There's no time to waste—up and at 'em!" George had us working hard and furiously. It didn't take me long to get used to acting with the cast on my wrist. I forgot about it pretty quickly. I kept glancing at Michael and George to see if I could detect any signs of anything having been settled. I couldn't.

At five o'clock George announced, "All right, kids—this was an excellent rehearsal. Let's make the rest of the rehearsals this week as good. See you tomorrow."

I hung back after the others left so I could talk with Michael. Just as I was about to ask if George had said anything yet, Thelma walked in. Michael looked up and smiled when he saw her. Then, behind her, in walked Mr. Abbot. My face must have looked as startled as I felt.

"Hello, Christy. Hello, Michael," Mr. Abbot said. "You look surprised to see me."

My mind raced. Oh, my gosh. George has told Mr. Abbot about Michael and he's been to the state orphanage to sign Michael in.

"Thelma and I were visiting a special person," Mr. Abbot continued.

You see, I was right, I thought. Wait—he said 'person.' He didn't say 'place.'

"Really?" I said. Maybe it was a social worker or some kind of official who would take Michael away. I was afraid to find out.

Thelma put her arm on Michael's shoulder and said, "We were visiting Justus, Michael's grandfather."

Michael's eyes widened. He opened his mouth, speechless. So did I.

"When we talked yesterday, Michael," George said, "I knew that I wanted very much to help you. But with my schedule in the theater, and all my trekking into the city, I can't take on the responsibility of looking after you."

That's what I was afraid of, I thought. Now he's probably turned the whole thing over to Mr. Abbot.

"Thelma and Bill Abbot have helped me out on more than one occasion. I knew they would share my concern for you," George said.

He said 'helped' and 'share my concern.' That sounded good. I looked at Michael. He still seemed bewildered by the whole scene.

Thelma gave Michael's shoulder a pat. "We went to visit Justus today to see how he was doing and to talk with him about the possibility of your staying with us until he's well enough to come home."

Michael looked from Thelma to Mr. Abbot and back to Thelma. "And what did he say?"

"He said he never expected to be away this long and he had no idea your mother wasn't with you. He said you should be with someone," Mr. Abbot said.

"But what about my mother? What if she calls or comes home?"

"We talked about that and thought we could arrange with the phone company to have your calls transferred to our house. And we can leave a note inside the house saying where you're staying in case she comes," Mr. Abbot said.

Michael smiled, then frowned. "But I have a bunch of cats."

"We'd love a bunch of cats. Bring them along," Thelma offered.

"Wow," Michael said, grinning. "Are you sure?"

"Very sure," Mr. Abbot nodded.

George picked up his jacket and script. "Then it's all settled? I'll help move some things if you need me."

"There's no time like the present," Mr. Abbot suggested. "But Michael, no special treatment in science. Understand? And stay in your seat until the class period is over!" Mr. Abbot laughed. I felt guilty that I used to call him Frogface.

"Sure. I have a good bit of catching up to do," Michael said. "Oh, do you mind if I don't bring all the cats? I'd like Christy to have one kitten."

"Oh, my gosh! Thanks! I think my parents will let me have one."

"Okay, I'll stop by tomorrow with the one I think you'll like. She's curious, always investigating. . . ." Michael smiled and pulled me aside. "You two will get along fine."

"Somehow I seem to get involved in things. I'm sor—"

Michael interrupted me. "Look, it's okay. You really did help. You're nice, and you care. That's a good way to be." He put both his hands on my shoulders. "Stay that way."

"Okay, Michael." I knew my face was red. "I'm really glad everything worked out." *Glad* was not the word for it—something ten times stronger than *relieved* was more like it.

* * *

The next day Michael dropped off my kitten. I named her Tinker Bell. Hazel and Beezer are having some adjustment problems. Tink's been batting them both with her paws and doesn't seem the least impressed by the fact that they were with us first. I gave Tink a one-size-fits-all flea collar which she likes about as little as I liked my first one-size-fits-all. I explained it's all a matter of getting used to . . . and maybe, if she thought about something—or someone—else for a bit, she'd find she could pass right through the uncomfortable stage almost without realizing it.

Twenty-five

Monday morning I stood by my locker.

Right 25 . . . left 16 . . . right 4 . . . PULL. I opened the door and gasped. Ants were everywhere! Parading over my books, in and out of my sweatshirt, up the locker walls and door.

Someone put an arm on my shoulder. I turned and faced Jeff, who was grinning at me. "Look at it this way, Chris. You have a head start on your bug collection."